ANGEL OF MERCY

*Also by*

# TONI ANDREWS

## BEG FOR MERCY

TONI ANDREWS

MERCY

ANGEL OF MERCY

MIRA®

**MIRA®**

ISBN-13: 978-0-7783-2547-5
ISBN-10:    0-7783-2547-4

ANGEL OF MERCY

For Maria Seager, who, by her example, reminds me what a friend can and should be.

# 1

Dear Angel of Mercy,
I know your busy watching over all the children.
But please can you help Mommy. She is sad all day.
We are in a new place now and Daddy does not
know where I am. But Mommy crys all day and
says she cant stop. I want too cry to but dont becuase
I know your watching and will help me soon.
Love, Grace

*I killed a guy last month.*

A horn sounded behind me, and I jumped. A
quick glance told me the light had turned green,
so I shook myself out of my reverie and put my
foot on the gas pedal. What passed for rush hour
in Balboa, California, wasn't over yet, and I was
interfering with the morning commute.

My office was only about two miles from my
beachfront apartment, and the route had less than

five traffic lights, so you'd think I'd be able to make it to work without getting sucked into a spiral of self-doubt and terror. *I killed Dominic. Deliberately.*

I wasn't afraid I'd be caught. I was pretty sure I had dodged that bullet. No, what woke me from a sound sleep almost every night was the cold dread that I would lose control again. Harm someone again. Put people I cared about in danger again. *I have no business doing this. I've got to stop kidding myself. I've got to—*

Yet another horn blared, and I jumped. Geeze, two trances in two lights. A new record.

Waving apologetically at the driver of the BMW hugging my bumper, I put the Honda into gear and sped out of his way. I probably should have walked or ridden my bicycle to work, as long as the perfect Southern California fall weather was holding out. But walking gave me too much time to think, something I was lately trying to avoid. And my one attempt to ride the bicycle with Cupcake in tow had been a disaster.

To distract myself as I drove the last few blocks to where I rented a parking space from a boat builder on the Lido Peninsula, I pondered the problem of Cupcake, who was standing in the backseat with his face squeezed against the window's narrow opening. I had acquired him less than a month ago—on the same day that I killed Dominic, actually—and I had sort of a joint-ownership agreement with my office manager. My apartment was bigger and had a patio along the boardwalk and the beach, so at the moment the one-hundred-and-thirty-five-pound rottweiler was bunking with me.

Cupcake, formerly known as Cujo, had been previously owned by a sleazeball who had not only thought it would be a great idea to have him trained to attack, but to respond to obscure voice commands. Nothing obvious like "kill" or "dismember," either. The two commands I had accidentally stumbled across so far were "nail file" and "bumblebee." Neither discovery had been made at a particularly convenient time, and I was living in fear that someone would say something like "hopscotch" and the otherwise mild-mannered canine would tear some innocent bystander's throat out.

I pulled into the parking space a few minutes early, got out and opened the back door. Cupcake obediently waited for the leash to be snapped onto his collar before tugging me toward the stairs to my office. He knew what was waiting behind the door marked *Mercedes Hollings, Hypnotherapy*.

"Cupcake!" Sukey squealed as if she hadn't

seen the mutt in months, when in fact she'd taken him for a run on the beach the previous evening. He put his big paws on her desk so that he looked more or less directly into her face. "How's my lover boy? Is he just the *best* boy in the whole wide world? Yes he is!" Her red curls jostled as she and Cupcake rubbed noses.

"Good morning, Mercy." Sukey managed to hand me a sheet of paper between sloppy dog kisses. I reviewed my day's appointments, noting an addition since the previous evening.

"Tiffany Wentworth. Did she say what she wants?"

"Nope. She said she'd rather talk to you about it. *Cupcake!*"

The enormous paws had knocked a book to the floor at my feet. I picked it up and read the cover. "*The Exciting World of Private Investigation.* When did you get this?"

"Last week." Sukey took the book out of my hands, her face coloring. She is sunshine to my darkness, in appearance as well as personality, and the flush of color on her freckled cheeks made her look like a naughty cherub.

"Since when are you interested in private investigation?" I tried to keep my amusement out of my voice.

Sukey shrugged, refusing to meet my gaze. "I thought it might come in handy."

"Handy how?" Needing caffeine, I went to the alcove and looked at the enormous coffee machine Sukey had purchased the previous week. It was made of chrome and had an assortment of unlabeled nozzles and levers. "Do you know how to work this thing?"

She came out from behind the desk and opened the cabinet door over the machine. "Sure." She took a bag of coffee beans from the cabinet and opened a hatch on top of the chrome monster. "I thought I might be able to help you find out about…you know."

"About what?" But she was right. I knew.

*About Dominic.* She didn't say it aloud, but I heard her just the same. *And about what you are.*

"I wish you wouldn't do that." I tried not to sound angry, but I was annoyed, and she knew it.

"So you say. But we need to talk about it."

I sighed heavily. "What do you want to talk about, Sukey?"

"About Dominic. About this telepathy stuff. About that *pressing* thing you do with your clients. Everything." She punched a button, and the electric coffee grinder started turning, emitting a high-pitched whine that prevented conversation.

It didn't matter, however, if the grinding sound drowned out voices. I didn't need to be able to hear Sukey for her to talk to me.

*You promised me we would try to find out more about it.* I heard her loud and clear, even the slightly petulant attitude.

I had only just discovered I was telepathic, so I wasn't sure whether Sukey's communications actually sounded the same as her voice, or if I unconsciously translated them into the tones I was accustomed to hearing. Dominic's messages had come through in his real voice, too. So far, I hadn't heard thoughts from anyone else. I guessed they would have to come from a stranger for me to find out about the voice thing.

The coffee grinder stopped whining, and the water began to trickle, sending up a fragrance that almost made me moan. Sukey got down two mugs, along with a heavy bowl that had Love Puppy painted on the side in bone-shaped letters.

She set the two mugs under the nozzles and pushed a button. Fresh coffee streamed, and I salivated like one of Pavlov's dogs. She filled Cupcake's bowl with water from the small sink next to the coffeemaker.

With a pointed expression on her face, she handed me the mug. I sighed again. She was right—I had promised. And there was no avoiding her, since I'd made her my office manager. I saw her every day, and now we had this crazy psychic connection. In fact, it was getting steadily stronger, had been since the day I'd saved her life. By killing Dominic. Who, incidentally, had been the one to show me I was telepathic in the first place. Unfortunately, that was achieved by putting some really nasty images in my head.

Sukey thought it was the coolest thing in the world. I wasn't nearly as enthusiastic, although it had saved me from having to invest in an intercom system for the office.

"Okay. After my last appointment this afternoon, maybe we can spend a little time working on it."

Sukey grinned like a happy six-year-old. "Can we do an experiment? I have some ideas."

I'd bet she had. "We'll see." She hummed to herself as she took one of the coffees back to her desk. We both knew she would talk me into whatever mad idea she had dreamed up.

And *I'm* the one who's supposed to be able to get anyone to do anything.

The door behind me opened, and I turned, expecting to see my first client of the day. A vaguely familiar man was standing in the doorway. He nodded at me, but his eyes moved toward the desk, lighting up when they found their target.

"Hi, Sukey. I got your note."

Sukey came around the desk. "Mercy, you know Carl, don't you? From downstairs?"

He held out a hand and, shaking it, I remembered where I'd met him: last month's opening reception for my hypnotherapy office. He worked for the graphic design firm in the large suite below ours.

"I asked Carl if he could help me with some Internet search stuff." She held up the private investigation book. "I'm on chapter four—'Your Computer is Your Sidekick.'"

A frisson of alarm almost soured my coffee. Sukey was the only person in the entire world who knew my secret, and I intended to keep it that way for as long as possible. I didn't like the idea of anyone looking over her shoulder.

Before I could think of a way to avert this potential disaster, the door opened again. This time it *was* my client. I ushered him into the therapy room, giving Sukey what I hoped was a significant look before closing the door. I shouldn't have bothered. She was already pulling the client chair around the desk so she and Carl could sit together, and she wasn't paying the least bit of attention to me.

What I do requires concentration. The sign on the door says *Hypnotherapy,* and my goals for each session are probably consistent with what I advertise. But I had an advantage my fellow graduates of the West Coast Institute for Healing Arts and Sciences did not. I called it *pressing.*

I asked enough questions to determine what the person really wanted to do—stop smoking, eat better, be patient with their teenaged kid—and instructed them to do it, but with an extra mental shove behind the words. When Sukey had asked me what it felt like, I told her it was like when a door sticks and you have to lean against it a little to get it open. Not very hard—just enough to overcome resistance.

My clients did what I told them to do. Exactly as they understood it. Without exception.

Which meant getting it wrong could be disastrous. Which was one of the reasons I was currently walking around with a cold piece of lead the size of a basketball in my stomach.

Happily, this morning's client was a slam dunk. I'm not sure I could have handled anything more complex. Ken was a fifty-year-old businessman recovering from his first heart attack, and he was having trouble sticking with the health regimen his cardiologist had prescribed. Guys like this were the reason I had opened my office. He needed help. I could help him. He got healthy. I got paid. No one got hurt.

Actually, getting paid hadn't been that much of a factor, although I did have an extortionate lease payment that was a big part of my monthly reality. I had been seeking a way to prove I wasn't fundamentally evil.

Killing Dominic hadn't helped.

After ending Ken's session with a reminder to renew his gym membership, I emerged from the therapy room to see if my newly added client had arrived. She hadn't.

Sukey excused herself from the lesson long enough to collect a payment, but Carl showed no sign of leaving and was making friends with Cupcake.

"So, what have you two been working on?"

Carl looked up while rubbing the wide plane that stretched between the silky ears. Cupcake moaned in appreciation.

"I've been showing her how to use site indexes. She's catching on really fast."

"For what sites?" I kept my tone neutral, not wanting to betray any motive other than idle curiosity.

"Any site. I'm showing her how to find out if

there are Web pages without a link in the regular user interfaces."

"Huh?" I wasn't completely computer illiterate, but I had no idea what he was talking about.

"You know when you go to a Web site and it has things you click on, depending on what you're trying to do? Like looking up your account information or something?"

"Sure."

"Well, in addition to the stuff you get to by clicking a link, they often have other pages that are attached to the site, that you can't get to that way. They're not secret or anything, just stuff that outside people don't usually need to see. The people that work for the company know the full IP addresses if they need to get to them."

I was sort of following him. "Go on."

"I was showing Sukey how to find out if a site had an index of all the associated pages, and how to find it and figure out if she wanted to see anything on those pages."

"Sounds good." It did. Certainly Carl's open face didn't indicate he and Sukey had been looking at anything he found puzzling. I probably shouldn't have worried. To the rest of the world, Sukey might appear to be a ditz. I knew better.

The front door opened and my new client

appeared, and I ushered her into the inner chamber, putting everything but the work at hand firmly from my mind.

"I need to stop making mistakes." Tiffany Wentworth's childlike voice was beginning to get on my nerves. Fifteen minutes into her session, I still couldn't understand why she was here.

"Tell me what kind of mistakes," I said, pressing slightly less gently than I had the last three times I'd given this instruction. It didn't change her answer.

"All kinds. I'm always screwing up."

I tried a different tack. "Do you remember the last mistake you made?"

"Yes."

"Tell me what it was." Now we could be getting somewhere.

"I took the wrong car yesterday."

I waited for further explanation, but none was forthcoming. Apparently, Tiffany felt the wrongness of her action was self-evident.

"Why was it the wrong car?"

"Because Stan wanted to drive it."

"Is Stan your husband?"

"Yes."

"So you took your husband's car, and he wanted to drive it?"

"Yes."

I thought about this. I supposed it was not uncommon for married couples to compete over the use of a favorite car, although if there was anyone who was less of an expert on marriage than I was, I didn't know who it would be. But the word "mistake" didn't seem to apply.

"Tiffany, why didn't you take your own car?"

"I don't have one."

This answer surprised me. Something about Tiffany said "wealth." I took a more critical look at her clothing and jewelry, but I didn't know one designer from another and wouldn't be able to tell a cheap cubic zirconium from the Hope Diamond.

Okay, back to the car issue. "How many cars does Stan have?"

"Five."

"Tell me about the driving arrangements between you and Stan. The type of cars, where you keep them, when you drive them, who does the driving."

I had finally taken the right track.

"Stan has a Range Rover and a Hummer that are parked in the driveway. He also has a Mercedes, a Ferrari and a Jaguar that he keeps in the garage. When we go out together, he drives. When I go out by myself, I can take any car except the Ferrari, because I don't know how to drive a stick shift."

"So yesterday you took the car Stan wanted to drive."

She nodded and did not wait for me to ask another question before going on. I guess my instruction about driving arrangements was still working.

"Yes, I took the Range Rover. I like to take it when I go shopping, because it's easy to get things in and out. I drove it to Ontario Mills."

"I see. But Stan had told you he wanted to drive the Range Rover, and you forgot. Is that what happened?" This didn't seem like much of a mistake to me. Not with four other cars at Stan's disposal.

"No, he didn't tell me."

This didn't make sense. "Then how were you supposed to know he wanted to take the Range Rover?"

"Because he told me he was playing golf with a Democrat."

This conversation, if you could call it that, was getting stranger by the moment. "Tell me," I began cautiously, "what playing golf with a… Democrat has to do with Stan driving the Range Rover."

"Normally he drives the Hummer when he goes to play golf. But yesterday he was playing golf with Harry Benson. Harry's a Democrat, and Stan says Democrats don't like Hummers because the governor drives one, and he's a Republican."

I almost laughed out loud, but sensed that Tiffany didn't see the absurdity of this speech at all.

"Was Stan upset with you?"

"Yes. He didn't know I took the Range Rover, because he was in the shower when I left. When he called me, I was already in Ontario, and he couldn't wait for me to get back, so he had to drive the Hummer, because he was supposed to pick everyone else up, and he wouldn't be able to fit all the golf clubs in any of the other cars."

Despite the strangely comical aspect of this story, I still didn't see how Tiffany had done anything that required hypnotherapy to overcome. I decided to tell her so, when she began to speak again.

"Stan wants Harry to help him get the city to approve his permit, but Harry said no. So Stan may not be able to build the new shopping center and then he won't make twenty-four million dollars, and it's my fault."

*Ah.* It was starting to make sense. Harold

Benson was the mayor of nearby Costa Mesa, and from what little I knew about him, he was an honest politician, if there is such a thing. Certainly not the sort of man whose influence was likely to be bought by a golf game, no matter what vehicle his host was driving.

Stan, no doubt frustrated by his inability to influence the mayor's decision, had probably come home and argued with Tiffany. He sounded like a real asshole, and he had no business blaming his wife because Benson didn't automatically make decisions in favor of developers like so many of his neighboring politicians.

I was about to tell Tiffany this when she leaned forward in her chair. She had chosen to sit in one of the comfortable armchairs rather than lie on the couch, and as her body came forward into the light, I noticed that the subtly-patterned scarf tied around her throat had loosened.

On the creamy skin of her neck, the outline of a handprint was clearly visible. I could see where the thumb had pressed against her throat under her chin and the index finger had dug beneath her hairline. I froze.

"Tiffany," I said very quietly, "please turn your head to the left."

Obediently, she followed my instruction, and I

could see the matching bruises on the opposite side. Someone had choked this woman and, by the color and distinct edges of the bruises, had done so recently. Like last night. Probably about the time she got home from Ontario Mills in the wrong car.

# 2

Dear Angel of Mercy,
Mommy said Daddy came to the other place to look for us but we aren't there and Rose told him to go away. Rose is nice and not afrayd of Daddy. She says he will go away but I no he wont ever stop looking for me because he loves me and I am his speshul girl. I told him I dont want to be speshul but he says I cant help it. Please, Angel, do not let Daddy find me and Mommy. Mommy says dont be afrayd but I am scared and I no Mommy is scared to but she says shes not.
Love, Grace

I'd developed the first and strongest of my special abilities just before puberty, and had spent almost twenty years trying to learn to control it. When I finally decided I was ready to use the press to help people, I knew there might be times when I was in over my head. This was one of them.

My first instinct was to command Tiffany to go home and tell Stan to shove his golf clubs, Range Rover and shopping-center deal up his ass. My second was to go with her and put some punch behind the suggestion.

I knew from sad experience that my instincts could not always be relied upon as a guide for the best course of action, but I was absolutely sure about one thing, and that was that the only real mistake Tiffany Wentworth was guilty of was marrying Stan.

*Mercy, is something wrong?* Sukey's voice in my head caused me to jump. Had I been thinking aloud? *Could* a telepath think aloud?

Sukey continued before I responded. *Mrs. Fellows has been waiting for ten minutes.*

Ah, Sukey was just being a good office manager. And since we didn't have that intercom…

*Tell her there's been an emergency, and I'll have to reschedule.*

*But…*

*Just do it, Sukey.* I cut the telepathic connection—something I had learned to do in order to keep Dominic out of my head—and returned my attention to where Tiffany sat looking at me with no expression.

"Tiffany, I want you to lie down on the sofa and take a little nap. You will be very comfortable and relaxed, okay?"

"Okay." Like a pliant child, she got up, crossed the room and settled onto the sofa with a soft sigh, looking even younger than she had moments before. I watched her, trying to figure out what to do next. Then I heard the outside door slam and figured the coast was probably clear in the outer office. I opened the connecting door and stepped into the reception area.

"Geeze, Mercy, I had to pretend to call you so I wouldn't look like a complete idiot just announcing there was some kind of emergency when I hadn't even spoken to you. I mean, she had been sitting there for ten minutes, and she knew I hadn't been on the phone and that you were—"

I cut Sukey off. "Can you call Hilda for me?"

Sukey blinked. "Hilda? Sure, but what does that have to do with…?" Seeing my expression, she trailed off. "There really *is* an emergency, isn't there?"

"I need someplace to stash Tiffany while I find out what to do next."

"Mrs. Wentworth? What's wrong?" Sukey had

managed to look up Hilda's number and dial the phone while we spoke, and she handed me the receiver just as the phone started to ring on the other end.

"Hello."

"Hilda, it's Mercy. I need a favor."

"What is it?" Hilda and I had become pretty good friends, but we weren't so close that her help was unconditional.

"I have a client who…well, she really shouldn't go home right now. I'll need a little time to make some phone calls, and I want to make sure she's somewhere safe in the meantime."

"Safe from what?" Sukey and Hilda spoke simultaneously.

"From her husband."

Silence greeted my statement, both on the other end of the line and in my office. I could hear the ticking of the cooling coffee maker.

"Of course you can bring her over," said Hilda. "Who are you going to call?"

"I don't know. I thought I would just go online and do a search for women's shelters or something."

"Well, maybe I can help you with that. There was this terrific woman who did a presentation at a fund-raising gala I went to a few months ago. I wrote them a big check, and I'm pretty sure I still have her business card. She runs a shelter somewhere around here, but I don't remember the name."

I felt a sense of relief. An expert was exactly what I needed. Before I started giving Tiffany advice that she *would* follow, I needed to know what that advice should be. "That would be great, Hilda. If you could look for it, I'll bring Tiffany over and call from there."

I hung up and turned to face Sukey. Her face was a mask of horror.

"Do you mean her husband has been beating her up?"

I shook my head. "I'm not sure. But he's been doing something. I stopped the session before I said something I would regret."

Sukey nodded. She understood, better than anyone, the damage my words could cause. "I know what *I* probably would have said."

"Yeah, well, I need to talk to a professional. Hilda says she knows someone."

"Do you want me to come with you?"

"No, you'll need to cancel my appointments for the rest of the day and take Cupcake home. Oh, and about tonight…"

She rolled her eyes. "I know, we'll have to

postpone my experiments. But don't worry, I'm not going to let you forget about them."

"I'm not worried." My dry tone was probably lost on her, but I had other things to think about.

I awakened Tiffany and told her we were going for a ride. When we got to the parking lot, I started to put her in my Honda, then thought better of it. She might have told Stan where she was going— I hadn't asked—and even if she hadn't, someone might recognize her car if we left it sitting out on the street.

At my instruction, she pointed out a Mercedes and gave me the keys. As I drove to Hilda's house, I couldn't help but enjoy the purr of the big engine and the smell of the leather. Even if I could afford it, I probably wouldn't buy an expensive car. To me, automobiles are transportation, period. But when I tapped the gas pedal while swerving to avoid running into a tourist, I had to admit I enjoyed the instant and effortless acceleration.

Hilda had a lot of cars, too, but that was because her late husband had been an auto dealer, and she was unwilling to part with anything he had driven. I figured she wouldn't mind moving one of the vehicles from the garage so the Mercedes would be out of sight.

"Tiffany, we are going to go visit my friend Hilda. You can feel safe in her house."

"Okay, I'll just call Stan and tell him where I am. He worries when he can't find me." She opened her purse, presumably to take out a cell phone.

*"No!"* I saw her stiffen and realized I had pressed too hard. And shouted, to boot. I kicked it back a notch—about four notches, actually—and gave her a press that was gentle, yet firm.

"You will not call Stan or anyone else until I say it's okay. All right, Tiffany?" I felt this was a safe enough command, until I knew more.

"All right." Her brow creased slightly with concern, but she would obey me.

She followed me docilely to Hilda's ornate front door, where I rang the bell and waited. When the door opened, Tiffany gave a little shriek and bolted back toward the car.

"What the—" Taking only a second to size up the sight that had frightened her, I went after Tiffany. "Stop!" This time I was careful not to press too hard, but even so, she practically skidded to a stop like a character in a cartoon. "It's okay, Tiffany, he's not dangerous. He's a friend. Come on back."

She obeyed me, but the expression on her face

told me she was doing so against her better judgment. Returning to the doorway, I took a much better look at the apparition before us.

An Hispanic man of about twenty-five stood in the doorway wearing nothing but prison tattoos and silk boxer shorts. Though not an especially big man, his muscles were well-defined and probably oiled, and he stood with that stance that allows men to push out their biceps as if by accident. His pirate's grin showed very white teeth, one of which had a gold cap, and he had a diamond in one ear. When I had told Tiffany he wasn't dangerous, it wasn't even close to the truth.

"Hey, *mamacita*. How you doin'?"

I shook my head in wonder. He didn't even look sheepish.

"Damn, Tino, put on some pants before you come to the door. What the hell are you doing at Hilda's house in your underwear, anyway?" The obvious answer occurred to me before he had the chance to respond, and I felt the hot blush rise into my face, even before Hilda came into view in the foyer. While she was fully dressed, her hair and makeup were not up to their usual immaculate standards, and she was barefoot.

"Good heavens, Tino, invite them in!" At her

appearance, Tino actually did look a little sheepish. Hilda was old enough to be his mother. Hell, Hilda probably had *shoes* older than Tino. And despite the best efforts of some world-class cosmetic surgeons, no one would mistake the fact that her first hot flash lay well in the past.

"Come in, come in. My name is Hilda, and you are…?" Hilda stopped, her mouth hanging open. "Tiffany *Wentworth?*"

"I'm sorry, have we met?" Tiffany held out her hand with a practiced gesture that made her look like one of the Stepford Wives.

"No, but I know your husband." Hilda took the hand. "Stanley Wentworth. I should have guessed. I never liked that son of a bitch."

Tiffany's eyebrows went up, and her mouth turned into a perfect circle. "But everyone likes Stan." Her puzzlement was genuine.

I intervened. "Tiffany, why don't you come with me to the front room? You can sit and watch the boats. You'll enjoy that."

Her face cleared. "Oh, yes, that would be nice." She followed me through the big house without protest.

I installed Tiffany on an enormous white sofa facing the picture windows, gave her a suggestion that watching the boats in Newport Harbor for a while would be very relaxing and pleasant, and that she should wait for me to return.

"What's wrong with her?" asked Tino as I entered the kitchen. He had a cup of coffee and was sitting at the breakfast nook.

"I never brought her out of the hypnotic trance," I said. This was not strictly true, but it was close enough. Even though Hilda was my occasional client and I had pressed Tino a couple of times in a pinch, neither of them knew the true nature of my "hypnosis." "As soon as I realized she was probably being abused, I stopped the session. I don't have any training dealing with battered women. I don't want to take the wrong action and make a mistake."

"Tell me where the asshole lives, and I'll take some action. There won't be no mistake about it, neither." Tino narrowed his eyes, and I suppressed a shudder. I liked Tino, and he could be very charming when he wanted to be. But I had never delved too deeply into his criminal background and was pretty sure I wouldn't like what I found if I did.

Hilda gave him a fond look, making me want to say "Ewww," then took a business card from the kitchen counter and handed it to me.

*Haven House,* it read. *Rosalee Jackson, Director.*

The address was a Santa Ana post-office box, and there was a phone number.

"Do you know where this place is?" I asked Hilda, who was loading pastries onto a plate. She shook her head.

"Somewhere in Fountain Valley, I think. They don't publish the address, because sometimes the husbands and boyfriends come looking for the women there."

"Makes sense. Do you mind if I use your phone to call?"

"Go ahead. I'll just take some snacks out to Tiffany." She vanished, and I took another look at Tino. He had put on a pair of jeans but was still shirtless. He was concentrating on a booklet open on the table before him, unselfconscious about the implications of his presence in Hilda's kitchen.

"Tino, I don't want to leave that Mercedes parked in the driveway. It's Stan's, and someone might recognize it." I had noticed the vanity plate—DVLOPR—on my way in. If Hilda knew Wentworth, others in this upscale neighborhood might, as well.

"Sure, I'll put it in the garage." He took the keys I offered and headed toward the side door. I wondered if his baby-blue Impala was currently occupying the space next to Hilda's Bentley.

"Haven House." The voice on the other end of the phone had a heavy Mexican accent.

"May I speak to Ms. Jackson, please?"

"Yus' a minute." There was a clunk as the receiver landed on a hard surface, and I heard muffled voices, then footsteps. After a few moments, the voice returned to the line.

"She say she be right wit' you." Another clunk and more muffled speech ensued.

I was about to give up when an out-of-breath woman said, "Rose Jackson."

"Ms. Jackson—" I began.

"Call me Rose." The interruption was swift.

"Uh, okay, then, Rose." I collected my thoughts. "Rose, I have your business card, and I'm wondering if you can help me."

"With what?" The tone wasn't rude, precisely, just to the point. A woman with a lot to do and not enough time in which to do it.

"My name is Mercy Hollings, and I'm a hypnotherapist."

"Are you calling to volunteer?"

"What? No. No, it's about a client of mine. She had a hypnotherapy session today, and I think—"

"Yes?" A tinge of impatience was beginning to come through.

"I think her husband is abusing her."

"Did she say that?"

"No, not exactly. But she said he was angry with her, and I noticed bruises on her neck."

"What kind of bruises?" The tone had sharpened.

"Hand-shaped. Like she had been choked."

"I see. Where is she now?"

"With me. I didn't think it was a good idea for her to go home until I figured out what's going on."

"And she agreed to that?"

"Sort of."

"What do you mean, sort of?" The tone was even sharper, and I was beginning to feel defensive. I was trying to help here, dammit, and this woman was interrogating me. I took a deep breath and reminded myself that this was about Tiffany, not me, and Rose just wanted to know what was going on.

"I never actually brought her out of the hypnotic trance. I was afraid she would bolt and go home before I could get to the bottom of the matter." Not precisely true, but close enough. "I have no experience with battered women. I didn't want to tell her…I didn't want to give any post-hypnotic suggestions that would be counterproductive."

"Damned smart of you."

*Was that a compliment?* I found myself wanting Rose's approval, which was not a familiar feeling for me. And I hadn't even met her.

"Anyway, I can't keep her in a trance forever, and I need to find out what to do next."

"Bring her here."

I hesitated. I had no idea what the shelter would be like, but I pictured a shabby house with too many beds in too small a space, and a flock of shrieking children being tended by chain-smoking women with bruised faces and hollow eyes. As a product of the foster-care system, I knew most social programs were vastly underfunded. I had spent a few nights in group homes where I wouldn't let Cupcake stay.

"Couldn't she just check into a hotel or something?"

"With what, her husband's credit cards?"

I saw my mistake immediately. If Tiffany didn't have any money of her own—and I doubted she did, since the cars belonged only to Stan—he would know exactly where she was the first time she spent a penny.

"All right, I see your point. There's no address on this card. Can you give me directions?"

She gave them to me readily enough. I had half

expected a request for a neutral rendezvous, with
passwords. The shelter was in a semi-industrial
neighborhood off the 405 freeway in Fountain
Valley, and I didn't think I would have any trouble
finding it. "I'll be there in about a half hour," I told
her, and after she told me she'd be waiting, I hung
up and went to get Tiffany.

I found her chatting with Hilda about a recent
yacht club event as if they were old friends at a
bridge luncheon.

"Hilda, I'm going to take Tiffany to meet your
friend Rose. I don't want to take her car, and I
think a convertible would be a bad idea. Can I
borrow the Suburban?"

"Why don't you let me drive you?"

I would need to pick my car up back at the
office anyway, so I took Hilda up on her offer. And
if Tiffany stayed at the shelter, Tino's new sugar
mama and I were going to have one hell of a conversation on the way back.


"Tiffany, answer all of Ms. Jackson's questions
as honestly and completely as you can."

If Rose thought my directive odd, she didn't
show it. She hadn't made any objections when I
sat down in the other chair in front of her desk. I
imagined that many women seeking her help

showed up with a friend or relative to provide moral support. She might not have been so amenable if she'd known the real reason I wanted to be present was to assess her competence before turning Tiffany over to her.

I needn't have worried. Rose Jackson was the very personification of competence. I would have bet it was one of the first words used by anyone describing her to others. She also managed to exude great gentleness, although I sensed a lot of toughness underneath. Even without a little help from me, Tiffany would probably have told Rose everything.

"Let me see your neck, Tiffany." Tiffany untied the scarf and let it fall to her lap. "Did your husband put those marks on you?"

"Yes. I made a mistake, and…"

"Shhh, honey. I don't care what you did, he doesn't have the right to put his hands on you like that."

"He didn't mean to." Tiffany's voice was almost a whisper.

"They never do."

I listened as Tiffany recited the details that made up the dynamic of her marriage. It was her job to be a perfect wife. She had understood this when Stan proposed. She just hadn't known that his definition of perfect included an ability to anticipate his every wish in advance. When she failed, he had no choice but to "correct" her.

Stan's corrections had included everything from verbal humiliation to beatings. He'd broken her wrist twice, blackened her eyes, raped her—Tiffany hadn't used the word, but her description left no doubt—and locked her in the hall closet for hours.

Tiffany described how, during the first such incident, she had gone through the sweaters and jackets on the hangers, trying to figure out in the darkness which ones were washable. She had used these garments to relieve her bursting bladder, then folded the wet items into a neat stack so the offending stains and odors were turned inside. When Stan had come home later and unlocked the door, he hadn't noticed, and she had been able to retrieve and launder them after he left for work the next day. She'd also put a small bucket and a flashlight in the closet as a precautionary measure. These items had proved helpful during later imprisonments.

Before leaving, I instructed Tiffany to be sure to do anything Rose advised. I gave Rose my card and asked her to call me.

"You're not running off to pay a visit to Mr.

Wentworth, are you?" Her pale brown eyes were penetrating.

"No, I'll leave him alone." *For now.*

"Good. When we go after him, it has to be by the book. Don't go doing anything that's going to give him ammunition in a legal case."

And she didn't even know me. I added perceptive to the list of adjectives in her description.

"I won't."

"Glad to hear it." Her expression softened. "You did the right thing by calling me. A lot of people in your position would try to handle matters on their own and likely as not make things worse. It's natural to want to defend the victim and go after the abuser, but it's usually not the best way in the long run."

I glanced at Tiffany, who was filling out a form. "What will happen next?"

"Well, she has *some* resources, so she's in a better position than a lot of women. She'll need to go to the police station and make a formal complaint, and tomorrow we'll have one of the lawyers who help us out file a TRO."

"TRO?"

"Temporary restraining order."

"I was under the impression those don't always do a lot of good."

She shrugged. "It's still a necessary step. Like I said, everything by the book. At least in this case we don't have to worry about issues with children. Those are always the worst."

# 3

Dear Angel of Mercy,
I hope you will come soon. I am not aloud to go outside to play becuase Daddy may come and look and then he wood see me. I told Mommy the other children shoud not play outside to becuase Daddy will look at them and maybe he will think one of them is speshul. But Mommy did not say anything and only crys so Angel please come and watch the other children too so they will be safe.
Love, Grace

"Hilda, he's a *felon*."

"Only technically. If you base his career choices on the environment in which he was raised, Tino's really more of...of an *entrepreneur*."

We were on our way back from the shelter. Only the fact that I didn't want our argument to distract

Hilda while she was negotiating rush-hour traffic on the 55 freeway kept me from pointing out how ludicrous it was to call a drug-dealing gang leader who, at any given time, carried enough illegal weaponry to supply a small revolution, an *entrepreneur.*

"Since when," I began cautiously, while watching to make sure she saw the motorcycle weaving between traffic on our left, "are you concerned with the social pressures placed on people growing up in the *barrio?*" When her husband was alive, he and Hilda had often hosted fundraisers for ultraconservative politicians who seemed to think the best thing to do about the blighted gang territories in Santa Ana and Anaheim was to bulldoze them and put up industrial parks and high-rise office buildings.

"I don't know how you can say such a thing, Mercy. I have always been very concerned about the plight of the less fortunate."

Her self-righteous tone irritated me, and I snapped back, "Yeah, but I'm pretty sure this is the first time you've expressed your concern by fucking one of them."

I knew I had gone too far the moment the comeback left my mouth. Hilda's cheeks colored, and her lips disappeared into a thin line. It's a good thing she was driving—if her hands had been free, she might have scratched my eyes out.

I didn't feel like apologizing. The fact that I had been the one to introduce Tino to Hilda lay under my annoyance like the smell of something that had just started to turn rotten. I had needed help, and needed it fast. I should probably have given a lot more thought to the potential consequences of inviting the leader of a Chicano street gang into my life and those of my friends.

But I'd never had friends before. And I'd never asked anyone for help, at least not since my adoptive parents had abandoned me to the tender mercies of the state almost twenty years earlier, so I suppose it wasn't surprising that the first time I combined vulnerability and companionship, there was some resultant fallout.

Hilda was driving too fast for the traffic conditions, and I had a feeling that if I looked straight at her I would be able to see her jaw muscles working. As accustomed to silence as I had become, the lack of conversation in the car was not comfortable. My hand itched to turn on the radio.

My cell phone rang, and for once, I was glad to hear the ring tone. So glad that I didn't check the display before answering.

"Hello."

"Hey, babe."

*Damn.* "Hi, Sam." *Would I have answered if I'd known it was him?* The thought flitted through my mind, but he spoke again before I had a chance to think about what it meant.

"Listen, I know you usually like to get a little more advance warning, but are you free for dinner tonight?"

"Tonight?" I had already told Sukey her telepathy experiment would have to be postponed. Wouldn't she be annoyed if I turned around and accepted a dinner date? Of course she wouldn't. Sukey was the most hopeless romantic of all time, and she thoroughly approved of Sam Falls.

"I had a craving for Middle Eastern food, and you mentioned you wanted to try that new restaurant."

I *had* said that, hadn't I? "Okay."

"Great. Pick you up at seven-thirty?"

I looked at my watch. "Yes, that'll be fine."

"See you then." He paused, and I waited for him to sign off. Instead, he said, "I miss you."

"Me too." It was out of my mouth before I had a chance to think about it. And it was true. *So why,* my annoying little inner voice asked me, *have you been avoiding him?*

"Glad to hear it. Bye." He ended the call, and the nasty little smell that had been my guilt over introducing Hilda and Tino was replaced by a much more cloying stench—that of denial and dishonesty.

Sam didn't know about my abilities, but he was too smart not to guess I knew more about Dominic's death than I was telling. He knew I was hiding something, and he didn't like it one bit. While I'd admitted I had a secret, I had also told him I needed a little time to work some things out before I gave him all the facts. He had accepted this, albeit with great reluctance. And, so far, he'd been patient. But it was pretty obvious his patience was wearing thin.

I had carefully steered clear of thinking about how Sam would feel if he knew that "work some things out" really meant "figure out if I'm human." I should have been looking for my birth parents, but I was terrified of who—or what—I would find.

By avoiding him, I was postponing the moment when he asked me if I was working on my as-of-yet unrevealed problem. And, because I respected him way too much to lie to him, I would have to tell him that I'd made no progress whatsoever. Zilch. *Nada*. And then he would…what? Have a tantrum? Storm out? I felt queasy at the thought.

I wasn't exactly scared of losing him. I was good at being alone. Hadn't I been that way most of my life? But Sam was…Sam. Even now, the thought of being in his presence, smelling his sea-salt and clean-man smell, watching his chambray-blue eyes light up when he smiled…

The car slowed, and I was pulled from my reverie to see a parade of brake lights ahead. I suppressed a groan. Everyone seemed to be heading to Balboa, even if it was more than six weeks after the end of the official season. A perfect day will do that. It just meant I would be stuck in the car with a pissed-off-and-not-speaking-to-me Hilda for another twenty minutes or so.

I was stung by guilt. Hilda had taken Tiffany in without question, driven us to Fountain Valley and waited in the car for an hour, and was now stuck in rush hour traffic. Only to be chastised about her love life for her trouble. I really did suck at this friendship thing.

I sighed. "I'm sorry, Hilda. What you and Tino do is your own affair. You're both over twenty-one, and it's really none of my business." A startling thought occurred to me. "Tino *is* over twenty-one, isn't he?"

"Mercy! He's twenty-seven!" She seemed more genuinely outraged at my underestimating his age than she had been at my calling him a criminal. Probably because there was no denying he *was* a criminal. Her eyebrows had risen—pretty amazing, when you considered the volume and frequency of her Botox injections—and, before I could stop myself, I laughed. Hard.

Hilda's eyebrows rose even higher, and I laughed louder. She turned her head toward me and opened her mouth, probably to call me an insensitive bitch, and I saw the flash of brake lights on the panel truck in front of us.

She saw them, too, and had to brake suddenly. This made me laugh even harder. "You'd better get over being mad at me, Hilda, or we're going to get in a wreck." I managed to gasp the words out between gales of laughter.

I saw her lips twitch, and then she, too, started to laugh.

"Oh, hell, it's no good. I have to pull over." She pulled the Suburban into the breakdown lane and put it into park, then succumbed completely to the hysteria.

I recovered first. "I'm really sorry, Hilda. It's just…if you could have seen the look on your face. It was as if I'd accused you of statutory rape."

"Well, you practically did." She wiped tears

from her cheeks. Her expression grew serious, but there was no longer any trace of anger in her tone. "Mercy, I know it's crazy. And I'm terribly afraid I look pathetic and ridiculous, fooling around with...well, you know. But he's just so *hot*. I haven't had this much fun since my first husband. And I've *never* had sex this good."

"Stop, before I get a mental picture I'll have to spend the rest of my life trying to get rid of," I said, ducking to avoid the half-serious slap she sent my way. "Just promise me you'll be careful. I mean, I like Tino, but—"

"Don't worry, I won't get my heart broken," said Hilda. "I know this can't really go anywhere."

"I was more worried about your jewelry or your artwork disappearing."

She waved a hand in dismissal. "It's all insured. And you can't think I'd give him the combination to the safe. No one's *that* hot."

As she put the big car back into drive and eased into the flow of traffic, I felt the laughter bubbling back up. Good old Hilda. She really could handle herself. Hell, I should probably be more worried about Tino.

"Hilda and *Tino?*" Sam's voice rose sharply enough that the man at the next table glanced over, although his gaze rapidly returned to the gyrations of the belly dancer who was weaving between the tables.

"Yup. I think he may be staying at her house." I took another sip of icy cold retsina. I don't usually gossip, but Sam would have found out sooner or later. And it was our second bottle of wine. Sam hadn't been helping me out much with it, either—he said it reminded him of turpentine. I had developed a taste for the resin-treated wine in college, when my closet-size apartment was directly above a Greek deli. Although the owners of this restaurant were from Tunisia, they advertised "Mediterranean Cuisine," so they included retsina on the wine list.

Sam shook his head and grinned, making my heartbeat speed up a little. He had the sexiest smile I had ever seen. Especially after not being with him for a couple of weeks and drinking just a bit too much wine.

He laughed. "That kid gets around. Where'd you meet him, anyway?"

"In a bar in Santa Ana, when I was looking for Dominic." *Shit.* The wine really *had* loosened my tongue. Our own personal elephant in the middle of the room, and I had to go and point it out.

Sam still smiled, but the sparkle had gone out

of his eyes, and he looked pensive. A waiter arrived and started gathering up some of the many small plates that filled our table. We had ordered the Oasis Feast, which didn't include an actual entrée.

"Could you bring more of the cheese things— what do you call them?" Maybe I could bring the focus of the evening back to the excellent food. *Why doesn't that damned belly dancer wiggle her pelvis on over here?* No heterosexual man would be able to concentrate on much else once she got all her substantial flesh moving to the beat.

"Yes, okay." The young man headed toward the kitchen. The restaurant was not particularly quiet, although neither the other patrons nor the piped-in whine of Middle Eastern pop music were loud enough to make conversation difficult. The rattling and clinking of the belly dancer's ornate belt and finger cymbals had moved to the opposite end of the room. I wanted to say something to restart the conversation, but I was drawing a blank. Sam had gotten very interested in his *maasems*— sort of a Tunisian egg roll—and was not looking at me.

The tinkling of the belly dancer's costume ceased, and more haunting music filled the air. It was rhythmic, but the pattern sounded too complex for dancing. "I don't think I've ever heard music like this before," I commented, glad for a new topic.

"It's *malouf.*"

"Ma-who?" I had a little more of the retsina.

"M-a-l-o-u-f," Sam spelled for me. "It's traditional Tunisian music. Do you like it?"

I listened to the multi-layered combination of voice, stringed instruments, flute and tinny drums. "I'm not sure. It's sort of…compelling. But it probably takes some getting used to."

This time his smile was genuine. "Sounds like this woman I know."

"Oh, yeah?" I gave him what I hoped was an arch look, and he wiggled his eyebrows. Crisis averted. For now.

Our smiling waiter reappeared. There was no sign of the savory tidbits I had requested.

"Could I have some more of the cheese pastries, please?" This time I made sure he was looking at me when I asked. I expected either a confirmation that they were on the way or an apology that he had forgotten. Instead, he smiled and said, "Yes, okay."

A suspicion arose. "Do you speak English?"

"Yes, very good." He nodded, and his smile grew even wider.

"Did you know that your hair is on fire?" I continued, my smile matching his.

"Yes, okay."

Sam stifled a laugh and took over the conversation. *"Men fadlek hal be'mkanik ehdar qet'at halwa beljobn le hathen alsayedah?"* he said, and I saw understanding light the waiter's eyes.

*"Belta' reed."* The young man moved off, this time with purpose.

"Was that Arabic?" I was surprised. To the best of my knowledge, Sam Falls had spent his entire pre-California life working on and around boats in South Florida.

"Yes."

I waited for further explanation, but he was scanning the remaining plates.

"Well?" I asked.

"Well, what?"

"Well, I wouldn't be surprised if you started speaking Spanish or something. I just didn't expect you to speak fluent Arabic."

"Oh, I'm far from fluent. Just a few phrases I learned here and there."

"Here and there in Key West?"

"There are Arabic speakers everywhere, you know. I worked with a few a long time ago." He shrugged. "You pick things up."

"Like an appreciation for traditional Tunisian music?"

"Yeah, like that."

Instead of our waiter, an older man appeared with a plate containing the tasty morsels that looked like tiny pie shells stuffed with a spiced cheese mixture.

"Here you go," he said, his accent light and pleasant. "My nephew says the gentleman speaks excellent Arabic. I thought I would introduce myself."

"Your nephew is being very kind. I'm only fluent when it comes to food."

"Well, that is a good thing in which to be fluent." The man smiled expansively. "Tell me, have you ever tasted *bokha?*"

"Not for years," said Sam.

"Will you not—" the man's gesture included me in the "you" "—join me in a glass?"

*Bokha,* it turned out, was liquor made from figs. The restaurant's owner, whose name turned out to be Hosni, poured it into beautiful tiny glasses reserved for the purpose. He had also produced a plate of sweet desserts that he insisted would be on the house.

"These—" he pointed to one side of the plate "—are *samsa.* They are made with almonds and sesame seeds—very authentic Tunisian. These others are *baklava,* made with pistachios. More Turkish than Tunisian, but I am addicted."

"I like the *samsa* better—do you use orange peel?" Sam picked up one of the delicate pastries and popped it into his mouth whole. His eyes closed in apparent ecstasy.

"Of course."

I tried one from each side of the plate. They were delicious but very sweet and, after the Oasis Feast, I was stuffed. I sipped the *bokha* instead.

"So, you have visited Tunisia?" Hosni's question was directed at both of us, and I shook my head, expecting Sam to do the same. To my surprise, he nodded.

"Yes, but only for a few days." A pot of coffee had arrived, and Sam drank from a small cup. As much as I am addicted to coffee, the murky brew looked too strong to drink at this hour. It might keep me awake, and I had to work in the morning.

"So where did you learn to speak Arabic?" The two men had exchanged a few polite phrases during the arrival of the desserts and after dinner-drinks, and although Sam had continued to protest that he had only the most rudimentary vocabulary, Hosni had insisted his accent was excellent.

"A few guys I worked with at the boatyard

when I was a teenager were from Morocco. At that age, you pick things up easily."

"Your accent does not seem very Moroccan." Hosni's comment sounded offhand, but Sam seemed eager to change the subject.

"Your English, on the other hand, is better than a lot of people born here. Have you been here a long time?"

"Eight years. But I went to school in England."

"Really? Your accent doesn't seem very English." Sam raised his cup, seeming to think he had scored a point, and Hosni chuckled.

"Touché, my new friend." He stood, then turned to me with a slight bow. "Now, if you will excuse me, I must see to the kitchen. I will leave the two of you to enjoy the rest of your evening."

The check had come and gone while we were eating dessert, and our glasses were empty.

"Are you ready to go?" Sam had risen to his feet.

"Sure. It's been a long day." I had told him a little about Tiffany and my visit to Haven House, without using names.

Sam beat me to the door and held it for me. I hadn't been accustomed to such courtesies before we started dating, and they still startled me a little. But Sam did it completely unselfconsciously, and that helped ease my discomfort. As I brushed past him, I smelled that unique Sam smell—salt air, clean man and pheromones. It made me want to turn my head into his shoulder and take a deep sniff. I held his arm loosely as we walked to his car, wanting it to be easy for him to pull from my grasp and put his arm around me. He didn't take the cue, but he did open my car door.

*Getting used to this stuff might not be too bad.* The wine and *bokha* had given me a pleasant glow, and I told myself I had imagined Sam's tension earlier. Certainly he seemed relaxed enough as I leaned back against the headrest and turned to watch his profile. He glanced at me, and I tried out a seductive look. He smiled, and I felt a familiar twinge in my groin. It had been over two weeks, and I got a sudden mental picture of long, tanned legs sliding in between cool, clean sheets. I shivered.

"We're almost there. Do you want me to put the heat on?"

"I'm not shivering because I'm cold."

The trip was short, and Sam pulled up in front of the boardwalk-level apartment I rented from the owners, who lived in the more spacious unit upstairs. He turned off the engine but made no move to get out of the car.

"Let's go in," I said, a little surprised by the huskiness of my own voice. "I'll light the fire." This meant hitting a wall switch, causing gas flames to whoosh over ceramic "logs," but it was still romantic in a kitschy sort of way.

"I'm pretty tired."

I felt my eyebrows rise in the dark, and a little chill began to intrude on my warm thoughts. "I won't keep you awake long." I tried to keep my tone light but wasn't sure I succeeded.

He turned to face me, and the brief glint of blue eyes was lost as a shadow covered the top of his face. "Look, Mercy, I thought I wanted to come in, but now I'm not sure that's such a good idea."

"What do you mean?" I couldn't make out the expression on his face, but I was a little bit afraid of what I would see there if I could.

He sighed. "You know what I mean. We never talk about it, and that's my fault, too, not just yours. But I was trying to give you time to bring it up on your own." He reached for my hand in the dark. "Your secret, Mercy. The one you're keeping from me. You promised you would tell me about it, and I think I've been pretty patient."

I straightened in my seat but managed not to pull my hand away. It took a lot of effort, but I kept my voice level. "I promised I would tell you everything as soon as I took care of something. I haven't done that yet."

"Have you even tried? You said it would take a little time and effort on your part, but it looks to me like your schedule is pretty damned full. If you're devoting any time to…to settling something, I can't figure out when you're doing it."

This time I did pull my hand away, and my voice wasn't perfectly even. Almost, but not quite. "I just opened my own business. I'm building my client base, and I can't start taking a bunch of time off. And I'm not the only one with secrets around here, Sam."

"What is that supposed to mean?"

It annoyed me that he sounded calmer than I did. Damned even-tempered, slow-talking sailor. Didn't he ever get riled up?

"You learned fluent Arabic from Moroccan *dock workers?* Tell me, Sam, was that before or after your visit to Tunisia?"

I winced at the sarcasm in my tone. He had asked me difficult questions, but he hadn't gotten nasty about it. I still couldn't see his expression, but there was something about his posture that told me I had made him angry or hurt his feelings or something. I really needed to work on my interpersonal skills.

I saw his shoulders relax, and, still calmly, he said, "Mercy, you've had a long and eventful day, and I have to get up very early in the morning to get Dad to his appointment with the new specialist. So why don't we just call it a night?"

"Always so damned reasonable, aren't you, Sam?" The words were out of my mouth before I could stop myself.

"I try to be. But you don't always make it easy."

I wanted to scream, to get out of the car and slam the door and stomp away like a child, but I wouldn't give him the satisfaction.

"Okay, Sam." I opened the car door, and the sudden illumination showed me that his face was still calm and his eyes gentle. He wasn't trying to make me feel bad or score points or prove he was right. A pang of guilt threatened to rise up and steal my anger, but I pushed it down—hard. "I'll talk to you soon. Thanks for dinner."

I closed the car door firmly, but you couldn't really call it a slam, and walked around the corner of the building toward the apartment's side door. I wanted to stop and lean against the wall, but if the inside lights didn't come on in a few seconds, Sam would know he had gotten to me. I managed to get the key into the lock without much of a struggle and reached for the light switch.

I heard an engine crank to life and the car drive away, probably a moment too soon for him to have noticed whether my house lights came on or not. I felt irrationally annoyed. Couldn't he *ever* behave badly? Just a little bit?

"Asshole," I said aloud, which was ridiculous. Sam Falls was the complete opposite of the label. I was just pissed because I knew damned well he was right. Absolutely, inarguably, fucking *right*.

# 4

Dear Angel of Mercy,
I dont know why you dont come becuase Im good
and pray very hard. Mommy wont talk hardly
none at all and sleeps all day but wakes up
becuase of the bad dreams. I have bad dreams to
but then I have good dreems and you come and
take me and Mommy to a nice house with pink
curtins and a doggy and a kitty and we are all
happy but then I wake up and its not reel.
Love, Grace

"Shit! Cupcake, hold still. *Sit!*" The rottweiler
dropped his butt to the sidewalk in instant com-
pliance, but every muscle under the sleek fur
trembled and twitched. He made a plaintive noise
and looked at me with a hurt expression.

"What's gotten into you?" I was on my way
back across the street from Alta Coffee. Sukey had

left a message that she would be arriving a little late, and the new coffeemaker had defeated me. After last night, I needed caffeine, but I shouldn't have tried to combine picking up a caramel mocha latte with taking Cupcake for his late-morning constitutional. Juggling a napalm-hot cup of coffee, a set of keys, a bag of dog shit and a leashed mutt the size of a small horse had resulted in splashing hot coffee on my hand.

"What's so interesting in that car?" I dropped the "courtesy bag" into a trash bin as I squinted to see through the tinted windshield of the sedan parked in front of my office building, but the glare from the bright California sun prevented me from seeing who was inside.

The passenger door opened and Sukey stepped out, solving the mystery of Cupcake's agitation. "Thanks again for breakfast. I'll call you if I can't figure out how to read any of this stuff." She was holding a large manila envelope.

She closed the door, and the car eased from the curb. I took pity on the twitching Cupcake, still technically in his sitting position but somehow managing to inch toward his beloved. "Oh, go ahead." In one leap, he was all over her, tongue lapping.

"How's my sweetheart?" asked Sukey in

crooning tones, managing to stroke the dog without dropping anything.

"Who was that?" I asked, gesturing toward the vanishing sedan.

"Detective Gerson. We had breakfast." She eyed the cup I was carrying. "Couldn't get the machine to work?"

I ignored her. "*Detective Gerson?* What are you doing having breakfast with a Newport Beach police detective?"

She didn't meet my eye. "It's part of my investigation of Dominic. I'm trying to get information on Rocko."

"Rocko?" I was confused. Rocko was Sukey's ex-boyfriend, and I was certain she was as happy about his having left town as I was. "Why are you looking for Rocko?"

"I'm not looking for him. I'm trying to find out about his past."

"Why?" I was starting to get a headache trying to follow Sukey's thinking, and my workday had hardly started. We arrived at the office door, and Sukey took the key from me to open it.

"Well, I remembered that Sam said a Newport Beach police detective showed him pictures the time Rocko ran the Balboa Island ferry into the dock and blew up Sam's gas pumps."

I had been on the scene only seconds after the incident, so I nodded. She continued, "That means he has a police record. Which means he's been in court, and there's got to be stuff about him on public record."

"Are we back on *The Exciting World of Private Investigation?*"

"Yup. It's so obvious. Dominic's identity was fake, so I can't trace him. But he told you he had known Rocko since they were both kids in foster care. And Rocko I can trace."

I felt mildly stunned. I knew Sukey was a lot smarter than I or anyone else usually gave her credit for, but she still caught me off guard from time to time.

While we talked, Sukey sat down at the desk and logged into my daily appointment calendar.

"Oh, I forgot to enter something," I told her. "I have a replacement client for the ten-thirty cancellation. Rosalee Jackson. She's a stop smoking."

"Since she's not here yet, I'll show you what I got from Bob."

"Bob?"

"Detective Gerson."

Was that a slight blush on her cheeks or just a trick of the light? Sukey put down her purse and opened the envelope while Cupcake abandoned us both for a long drink of water. He had peed on every bush, blade of grass and crack in the sidewalk on the short walk to and from the coffee house and needed to refill his tank.

"What is all this stuff?"

"It's Rocko's 'sheet.' And copies of whatever else they had on file."

"You got Detective Gerson to hand all this stuff over after one breakfast?"

"It was breakfast and a phone call yesterday afternoon. Hey, you're not the only one around here who can be persuasive. You know I give great phone." She continued to spread documents over the top of the desk. In one of them a mug shot showed an unsmiling face. "Most of this stuff's public record, anyway. He's just saving me the trouble of having to track it all down on my own."

"Nice of him."

"Yes." Sukey picked up the grainy copy of Rocko's mug shot and gave it an almost-fond look. "Too bad he turned out to be such an asshole. He sure is beef!" She sighed and put the picture back down.

I had never seen the attraction myself, but Sukey had been crazy about the guy. Right up until he had given her a heroin overdose and abandoned her in the Hoag Hospital emergency room parking lot.

I picked up an arrest record from 1997. Scanning the form for some explanation of the crime, I finally found the notation "breaking and entering." "Do you think you'll find anything here? The way Dominic talked, their connection went back to childhood."

"Bob, I mean Detective Gerson, said Rocko had a juvenile record, but you need a court order to get that. But he had another idea."

"What's that?"

"I told him there was a good chance Rocko was in the California state foster-care system. Bob has a relative who's pretty high up in Family Services, and he might be able to find out what families or group homes Rocko was placed with."

"No kidding." I was impressed. "Bob—I-mean-Detective—Gerson is willing to do all this for you on the strength of one phone call and a breakfast meeting?"

This time the blush was not my imagination. "Well, I did agree to meet him for happy hour tomorrow. But I did that because he seems nice, not because he's getting information for me."

"Sukey…"

"I know, I know. Don't worry, Mercy, I don't fall for every guy who wants to buy me a drink anymore. You know that better than anyone."

After the Rocko heroin-overdose incident, I had felt it prudent to apply my abilities to Sukey's issues around men and self-esteem. She was no pushover, not anymore.

The door opened, and Rose Jackson came in. "Sorry I'm late," she said. "I had trouble finding a place to park."

"That's my only problem with this location," I told her. "Unless you count the extra rent for the privilege of having a Newport Beach zip code. And you're not late, you're right on time." I turned to Sukey. "This is Ms. Jackson. We'll go ahead and start, and she can do the paperwork afterward."

"I told you, call me Rose," she said as I ushered her into the inner office. "The women at the shelter call me Ms. Jackson, and I'm okay with that, because a lot of them need to see a woman in an authority position. But I'd rather you used my first name."

"Good. And I'm Mercy." I gestured to the couch. "Tell me why you're here, Rose."

"Not much to tell. I need to quit smoking. Actually, I've quit about a thousand times, it just never took." She took a pack of cigarettes out of her handbag, looked at it and threw it in the trash can. "I don't even like smoking anymore. And I hate how it makes my hair smell. African American women can't go washing their hair every day, you know. And we're something like twice as likely to die of lung cancer as white women."

I nodded. "Sounds like you're convinced." Even with something as seemingly obvious as a quit-smoking case, I always had to make sure I understood my clients' motives before proceeding. The old expression—Be careful what you wish for—held special meaning for me. For example, when I'd pressed Hilda to stop drinking as part of her weight loss program, it had turned her into a complete teetotaler. I didn't think she was suffering, but I had felt a little guilty when I saw her turn down a glass of champagne from some friends who were celebrating their fiftieth wedding anniversary. I might have to do a little follow-up with her at a future date.

Rose's session went routinely, and twenty-five minutes later I was asking her how she felt.

"Good. Relaxed." She blinked and looked around. "And I know it's probably too soon to tell, but I think it worked." She tilted her head to one side, eyeing me speculatively. "You're good, aren't you?"

"I hope so." I opened the door to the front

room, preparing to turn her over to Sukey for the paperwork.

Rose didn't head through the door immediately. "What time do you generally go to lunch? I have a couple of stops to make while I'm in the neighborhood, but I wonder if you'd like to join me afterward."

I was mildly surprised. "I don't schedule any appointments between one and two-thirty. Did you have a place in mind?"

"Yeah, I like to go to the Crab Cooker whenever I have a reason to be down here. Sometimes I actually dream about those oyster kabobs."

"I feel the same way about the Manhattan clam chowder. Can I meet you there a few minutes after one?"

"Perfect." She turned and took a clipboard from a waiting Sukey, and I gestured my next client into the office.

              •

The Crab Cooker was always boisterous, even at lunchtime. The food was good enough that a steady stream of customers didn't mind sharing picnic tables with strangers and eating from paper plates, even if the prices didn't reflect the modest ambiance. By the time we finished eating, the crowd had thinned and the din dropped to a dull roar.

"I'd keep eating, but then I'd have to go home and change into my fat pants." Rose wiped her mouth and patted her belly. She was a big woman but wore her weight well. "I need to get back to Haven House and get some work done—we've got evening groups tonight."

"Evening groups?" I waved away the waitress who was trying to refill my iced tea.

"We have group therapy of one kind or another every day," explained Rose, "but some of the volunteer therapists can only come in the evening. So we hold sessions after dinner on two nights every week."

"I see." I felt a little nervous. Rose was eyeing me with that same speculative look I had seen immediately after her session that morning.

"We have one-on-one therapy, too, for some of the residents who have more serious problems."

"What kinds of problems?" I had a feeling I wasn't going to like where this conversation was going, but she was drawing me in. She had regaled me with surprisingly funny anecdotes about shelter life while we ate. Lulling me into a false sense of security, no doubt.

"Mostly self-esteem. Some of these women are so beaten down—literally and figuratively—by the time they come to us that they actually think they deserve to be abused. They were abused as children. Their fathers beat their mothers. Their own brothers and cousins raped them." She let out a heavy sigh. "That's why so many of them go right back to the abusive situation. They think that's how the world is supposed to work."

"It sounds discouraging."

She looked surprised. "I didn't mean for it to. I love what I do. Sure, we lose a lot of them. But when we win one, it makes up for everything." She leaned toward me, eyes bright. "Do you know what it's like to see someone come alive after living in a fog for years? It's like watching a flower bloom out of solid concrete."

"Sounds like you love your job."

"I truly do." She leaned back, eyes still on me. "And I think you could help me."

Ah, here it was. "Look Rose, I don't think—"

She raised her hands, interrupting. "Just hear me out. I saw the way Tiffany Wentworth trusted you and did what you asked, even though you had only met her that day. And here I am, sitting here after finishing a big meal, and I have absolutely no desire for a cigarette."

She waved away my hand as I reached for the check, picking it up herself. "I don't know how you do it, but you have a way of making people believe they can do things. And that's something these women desperately need—to *believe* it's possible to change things. To *believe* they can be something. To *believe* they have choices."

"I don't know, Rose. I'm just starting my own business, and I have a lot of other things going on in my life right now." I heard the weakness of my own words, pale and feeble in the face of her fervor.

"Mercy, I'm just talking about an hour or two a week. Let me pick out one or two women who I think you could help, and you give it a try. If you don't like it, or scheduling becomes too big a problem, you can always quit." She put a few bills on top of the check and grinned at me. "It's not like I plan on paying you."

I grinned back. I couldn't help it. "You said a couple of hours. When? What days of the week?"

Her smile got broader, because she knew she had won. "You tell me. The shelter's clients are there 24-7, so we can do it pretty much any time you want, other than meal times."

We walked back to our respective cars, discussing possible time slots, and agreed that I would come by Haven House the following evening after my last appointment. As I watched her speed off in her VW Bug, a thought that had been tickling the back of my mind finally found its way to the fore-front.

*Is this just another way to avoid looking into my origins?* I didn't think so. But I wasn't at all sure Sam Falls was going to agree.

"I'm going to have you work with Chantal Dupree tonight, Mercy. She's been here two weeks, and she's thinking about going back to her husband." Rose had wasted no time in leading me to a small sitting room furnished with clean, if shabby, furniture.

"And he abuses her?"

"Yep. He's broken her arm, her ribs and her collarbone, and hit her in the face and on the head so many times she's practically deaf in one ear. But so far he's never hit the three kids—according to her—and she's got it in her head they need their father."

"Do they?" It sounded like a stupid question as soon as it was out of my mouth, but I always seemed to drop my guard around Rose.

She just shook her head. "It's not unheard of for a man who abuses his wife to have a good re-lationship with his kids, at least on the surface. But that's almost worse for the children, because they start to see the beatings as normal, even as something their mother deserves. 'Why do you always make Daddy so mad, Mommy?' At the same time, they can never really trust their father, because they're always wondering when it's going to be their turn."

She sighed. "Which it almost always is, eventually. Someone who solves his problems with his fists isn't going to be selective in the long run."

I nodded. "Okay, what do you want me to do?"

She laughed. "Whatever it is you do, child. Chantal needs to know she's worth something. That she *is* somebody. And that she doesn't have to go back to that animal—*can't* go back to him, not if she wants to keep those children safe."

I was starting to feel a little excited. I had a feeling Rose had that effect on people. A woman in a pink sweat suit passed the door to the sitting room, and Rose called to her.

"Marisol, would you tell Chantal that Ms. Hollings is ready for her?"

"*Sí*, Ms. Jackson."

As we waited, I asked, "How is Tiffany? Can I see her?"

"She's not here."

I was alarmed. "She didn't go back to Stan!"

"No, no," she soothed. "Her sister came and picked her up. Tiffany is fortunate in that she has resources. Her family isn't rich, but they can take care of her until she's on her feet. They had no idea Stan was abusing her, and they were furious."

"What's going to happen to him?"

She smiled painfully. "Probably nothing. I don't think she's going to press charges."

*"What?"* I couldn't believe it. "Why the hell not?"

"Because Tiffany's husband is a very rich man with a lot of resources. He can afford the best lawyers in Southern California, and anyone who watches *Court TV* can tell you what that means." She slumped back in her chair. "There were no witnesses to the abuse, and he usually didn't hurt her so badly that she had to go to the hospital."

"So he gets away with it." Maybe I'd take a page from Tino's book and pay him a little personal visit.

"Luckily for Tiffany, even the hint of scandal could hurt Stan's business, so he probably won't fight a divorce and she'll end up getting a decent settlement, even though he made most of his money before they were married."

"But he could do the same thing to some other woman." I was still furious.

"And he probably will. That's just the way it is sometimes, Mercy." She leaned forward and took my hand. "But you got Tiffany out, and you can feel good about that. After the divorce, she'll have a little money, and she'll be able to make a start. And maybe the next wife will call the police and get Stan's ass thrown in jail."

"Or maybe he'll be crossing Pacific Coast Highway and get hit by a bus."

"One can only hope." This time Rose's grin wasn't forced.

"Excuse me," said a soft voice, and I looked up to meet Chantal Dupree. *Good God, she has three children?* She didn't look more than twenty.

"Chantal, this is Ms. Hollings." The name sounded strange to me, but Rose had told me it was better to use the title. "I'll leave you two to get acquainted."

She left, and Chantal sat down, looking at me like a scared deer. "You gonna hypnotize me?" She said the word carefully, as if she had been practicing the pronunciation.

"In a few minutes, yes. Are you afraid?" She obviously was.

"Deena say you get hypnotized, they make you do things. Whatever they want. And you can get a post…post—" She struggled for the term, and I supplied it.

"A post-hypnotic suggestion."

"Yeah, that thing. You do that?" Her eyes were

like saucers. "Make a person do things, when they ain't even hypnotized anymore?"

"Sometimes, yes. Like if someone comes to see me to lose weight, I might suggest they would enjoy eating healthy food and exercising."

She chewed on that for a moment. "That don't sound so bad. It just like, what they need to do."

"That's right."

"So what you gonna tell me to do?"

I hid a smile. Few of my multimillionaire clients had given me a more rigorous pre-session interview. "I don't know yet. Not until I find out what *you* need."

"I *need* to take care of my babies." She had stopped sounding scared.

I nodded. "Then it will probably be something about that."

She frowned, then seemed to make up her mind. "Okay. You go ahead, then. Want me to lie down or something?"

"If you want to."

She got up and scrutinized the sofa, which looked lumpy and uncomfortable to me but must have passed her inspection, because she flopped down and rearranged some threadbare pillows under her head. "Okay, I'm ready."

I took her through the normal opening, using a

light press to instruct her to be completely relaxed and comfortable and, most important, to tell me the full truth. In my experience, even clients with very straightforward goals would embellish or abridge the truth without this command.

I had had some apprehension about this session, because domestic abuse was a new topic for me. But self-esteem wasn't—I had often employed some light suggestions about deserving happiness with some of my clients who were failing at their goals because they lacked confidence. And my most successful self-esteem case brightened my every day. Sukey had been a positive force in my life since the day she decided she would become my best friend whether I liked it or not. I hadn't had a close friend since adolescence, and she had not cared one whit for my reluctance.

But since the time I had pressed her to appreciate her own value as much as she did that of everyone around her, it had been wonderful to watch her stretch to reach for her full potential. Thinking about this, I took a deep breath and began.

"Chantal, you know you are a good person and you deserve to be treated with respect. Do you believe you deserve to be treated with respect?"

"I believe it." Chantal sighed like a happy child.

I was really going to love this job.

# 5

Dear Angel of Mercy,
If you cant come soon could you please send me a freind. I had a freind Jimmy but Daddy sayed I could not play with him becuase I could only be Daddy's freind becuase he wood be lonley and sad if I had someone else to play with. But Daddy is not here so maybe I could have a freind now since Mommy wont talk and I am afrayd to talk to grown ups excetp you.
Love, Grace


"Happy Birthday, dear Grant. Happy Birthday to you," I sang along from a spot near an exit, trying to keep my voice low. Hilda's house was full of people I didn't know or want to know. She knew I hated Newport Beach society events, but she had used my respect for Grant to generate enough guilt to get me in the door.

Sukey had, of course, led the singing and was now standing at Grant's elbow. "Make a wish, Grant!" Sukey loved this shit.

Grant's white head dipped below the surrounding crowd, disappearing from my view as he bent to blow out the candles. Thunderous applause arose, as if blowing out a few candles was some kind of major achievement.

I felt a presence at my side and turned to find Tino. "Hey, mama."

"Hey, Tino." I managed not to do a double take at his outfit. He was Balboa Bay Club cool, sporting a raw-silk summer suit that had probably cost more than my car. That outfit would have gotten him killed in the *barrios* of Santa Ana, not least of all because it hid his tattoos. He looked like a young Antonio Banderas.

"I look good, right?" The grin almost shattered the illusion as his gold tooth winked, only to be quickly outshone by the glittering watch revealed by the fall of his cuff as he lifted a Corona to his lips. "Caught you lookin'." He winked, and I laughed.

"Yeah, Tino, you're hot." A uniformed waiter walked by with a tray of champagne, but I had my eye on Tino's beer. "You know where I can get one of those Coronas?"

"Yeah, they're in the kitchen. I'll get you one."

"I'll come with you."

Within moments we were seated at the breakfast nook, ice cold bottles starting to drip condensation on the table in front of us. We had to stay out of the way of the caterers, who were using the oven to warm canapés and the counters to rotate trays. A uniformed Hispanic woman placed a small plate with sliced limes in front of us, giving Tino an appreciative glance. He didn't notice and played with his beer.

"This doesn't seem much like your scene, Tino." The beer was cold and delicious, just exactly what I wanted.

"Yeah, I know. But Hilda wanted me to be here, and Grant is my *vato.*"

"*Vato?*"

"You know, my homeboy—my homey, man."

I managed not to choke on my beer at this description of the sixty-seven-year-old millionaire retiree, but asked, "You're hanging out with Grant these days? What's up with that?"

Tino looked at everything except me. Was he *blushing?* "Yeah, well, you know, he's helping me out with some stuff."

"What stuff?"

Tino shrugged. "Stuff."

I stared at him, and he must have figured out I wasn't going to let it go, because he leaned back and opened a small drawer behind the nook. He took out a pile of paperwork and threw it on the table in front of me.

I picked up a book nestled in the pile. It bristled with Post-it notes. *Guaranteed GED Success: Pass the Tests or Your Money Back.* I was surprised.

"You never graduated from high school?"

A little hostility flashed in his voice. "Hey, man, I was busy. You know, stayin' alive?"

I raised my hands in a gesture of peace. "I'm not judging. I almost didn't get through myself. I was too occupied with running away from foster homes. I was just surprised. You're obviously a smart guy."

The ego stroke had the desired effect on his ruffled feathers. "Yeah, well, I just stopped going. No big deal. But Grant, man, he's all over me about this. Says if I don't want to run a gang my whole life, I gotta do it."

"You don't? Want to run the gang, I mean?"

He shrugged again. "Average life expectancy for guys like me ain't too good, if you know what I mean. And, like, you can get a nice car, wear some good jewelry, stuff like that. But nothin' like this."

He waved his beer bottle in the direction of the window, and I glanced out at the nighttime view of the harbor, brightly illuminated by the lights from houses on the other side of the bay and the running lights of a few boats. The spot-lit palm trees arching over the steps down to Hilda's pier looked like an advertisement for the good life.

"The people who own these houses have a lot more going for them than a high-school diploma," I said, then winced at my tone. Tino wanting to get out of the gangs was a good thing, and I shouldn't discourage him. I needn't have worried.

"I know *that*," he said, as if speaking to an idiot child. "They're doctors and lawyers and do investments and real estate shit—whatever. But Grant says you gotta start somewhere. He says there's a lot of ways to get rich, but if you don't do it legal, they just find a way to take it away from you. You need, like, tax shelters and shit."

This was surreal. I had never considered I might make enough money to need to know about tax shelters. Now I was discussing their importance with a Chicano gangster.

"Hey, you two."

I looked up to see Sam in the doorway. He was smiling. Good. Maybe it was time to mend fences. I smiled back. "Hey yourself."

"Got any more of those Coronas?"

I gestured toward the fridge, and he took one out.

"Grant was looking for you," he said, nodding at Tino. "Someone he wants you to meet."

"Thanks, bro." Tino edged out of the seat and passed Sam on his way out, the two of them doing some sort of complicated handshake and slap ritual. So Grant was Tino's homey and Sam was his "bro."

"I can't keep up with that guy," I said, nodding at Tino's departing back.

"He does move fast." Grinning, he took the seat Tino had vacated. "You look great."

"Thanks." I was wearing a deep red sweater Sukey had picked out. She was making gradual inroads on "the black hole," as she called my closet, but I had so far resisted her attempts to get me to buy a set of hot rollers. "So do you. Although—" I nodded toward the door through which Tino had vanished "—you're not as pretty as Tino."

He laughed aloud. "No one is. The Loyal Order are all atwitter."

This was a Grant reference—he called the coterie of Balboa Bay Club wealthy widows "The Loyal Order of Gray Pussies." Between them, these women had put the children of more cosmetic surgeons through college than the National Merit Scholarship Association. And if they did have any gray hair, it definitely wasn't on their well-coiffed heads. As one of the few bachelors old enough and rich enough to catch their interest, Grant was in the rare position to know whether their collars matched their cuffs.

It felt good, sitting there bantering with Sam. I searched his face for any sign of hostility about the night of our date and found none. I owed him an apology.

"Sam, about the other night…"

He put a hand over mine, which was toying with the plate of limes. "It's okay. I know you'll tell me when you're ready. In the meantime, I just have to trust you're doing what you need to do."

I sighed. If only he weren't so perfect to look at. Not perfect in the classical sense—his aristocratic nose had been broken, and the sun had put deep creases in his face. But perfect for me—I was fascinated by every line and bump, and wanted to run my fingers over his skin.

He trusted me, and I wasn't doing anything to earn that trust.

*But Sukey is.* The thought heartened me. Sukey was trying to find out where Dominic came from, through Rocko. And Dominic was—had been—like me. Whatever that meant. Could I tell Sam we, as in Sukey, had made a small start?

"Listen, tomorrow night is the full moon. Want to take an evening sail?" he asked.

"Yes" was almost out of my mouth before I remembered. I saw my own changing expression reflected on his face as I spoke. "I can't. There's something I have to do."

"Something…to do with your secret?" His voice sounded careful, as if he wanted to know but didn't want to seem to be pressuring me.

"No. I volunteered to do some counseling at a battered women's shelter. Tomorrow's my second night."

There was a beat of silence, then he said, "I see."

"What does that mean?" I felt defensiveness rising but was helpless to stop it.

"It doesn't mean anything. I'm just a little surprised, that's all."

"Why should it surprise you?" Was I trying to pick a fight?

"Well, you're always saying how busy you are and how little free time you have. I'm just surprised you would take on another commitment."

"Instead of working on my personal business."

"You said it, not me." His voice was neutral, but mine was starting to get sharp.

"Sam, it's only a couple of hours a week. And it's important."

He looked down at his beer, rolling the bottle between his hands. "Yes, I suppose it is. And if I suggest you shouldn't do it, then I'm automatically the bad guy."

I snorted. "Sam, you may be a lot of things, but I doubt you've ever been the bad guy."

"You'd be surprised."

"Yeah, I would."

He looked at me, then back at his beer. He sighed and slid out of the seat, and stared down at me. I resisted looking back, keeping my eyes on the table.

"I hope your volunteer work goes well, but I'll miss you on the water." He didn't move, so I tilted my head up to look at him. His expression was inscrutable.

"I'm going to find Grant and say good-night, then take off. Good night, Mercy." He sauntered out of the kitchen, and I watched him go, searching his body language for signs of tension. I didn't find any.

I sighed. As usual, he had robbed me of the right to be mad at him. Reasonable, reasonable, reasonable. If just once he would behave badly…

A scream, shrill and very close, cut through my thoughts. The uniformed caterers in the kitchen froze, faces turned toward the door. A familiar voice rang out.

It was Sukey. "Cupcake, *no!* Let him go right now! Sit. *Sit!*"

*"Shit!"* I was through the dining area and into the great room so fast I didn't remember getting there. It was as I feared.

A well-dressed man of about Grant's age lay on the floor, where a white-haired woman—presumably the source of the scream—fluttered over him. Cupcake sat next to them, his ass glued to the marble tile by the sit command.

"Howard, are you okay?" The woman's voice had an hysterical tinge. "Oh, God, he's bleeding. Someone call 9-1-1."

I started to dig my cell phone out of my pocket to do just that when Howard sat up. "Dolores, I'm fine. I'm not bleeding, I just spilled my Bloody Mary."

"Oh, I am so sorry," said Sukey, who was trying to get between Dolores and Howard in order to mop up the tomato juice on the latter's shirtfront. "I don't know what got into Cupcake. He's really a very good dog. I'll get your shirt cleaned for you, of course."

Howard waved her away. "Don't worry about it, my dear." Aided by Dolores and Sukey, he regained his feet. "And he does seem like a good dog. Very friendly earlier. Then all of a sudden, he just leapt up and grabbed me by the throat with his teeth."

"Really?" It was Hilda. "Who was talking to you? What did they say?"

"Wha-what?" Howard was obviously confused by the question.

It was time for me to intervene. "I'm sorry, we haven't met." I shouldered past Hilda. "I'm Mercy, and I need to apologize for my dog."

"*Our* dog," contributed Sukey, but I ignored her.

"His former owner had him trained to voice commands, but I never found out what they all were. I'm working on a list."

"We all are," said Hilda. "So we need to find out what someone said just before Cupcake jumped on you."

Tino, who had come up during the conversation, joined in. "His throat ain't bleeding, so it must be some kind of 'hold' command. If it had been a 'kill' word…"

"Yes, thank you, Tino," I overrode him. "I'm very sorry, but Hilda is right. It would be really helpful if we could figure out what command set him off."

"What, another Cupcake word?" Grant spoke from behind me. "And I missed it? Damn! Who was talking?"

"I was," volunteered a tall man in a Hawaiian shirt. "I was talking about cars."

"Cars? Mercy, have we tried car names?"

I shook my head. "No, Grant, we haven't. But I really don't think this is the place…"

Ignoring me, Grant turned to Cupcake. "Ferrari. Maserati. Volkswagen." The big dog looked up at him, listening, but didn't react.

"I see what you're doing," said Howard. He turned to Hawaiian shirt guy. "What kind of cars were you talking about?"

The guy blinked. "Several. But more about engines and performance than actual models." Getting interested, he turned toward the dog as well. "Er…turbo. Cylinder. Carburetor." Cupcake panted on.

I tried reason. "Hey, you guys, have you considered that if you come up with the right word, he's going to jump on someone again?"

"It was just a hold command, Mercy," said Grant. "It would be very useful to know it." He turned back to the growing circle of participants, now taking turns calling out words like spark plug and fuel injector. "But you all might want to set your drinks down."

"Convertible," said Tino, placing his beer on an end table, sans coaster. "Roadster."

"Come on, Dolores, let's get you a fresh cocktail," said Hilda. "I hope you're not too upset."

"Well, Howard's not hurt," said Dolores, albeit a little shakily. "And at least something interesting is happening at this party. They're usually so dull."

The two women headed toward the kitchen, and I stood helplessly in the middle of the great room, feeling I should somehow take control of the situation.

"Mercy, can I talk to you?" Sukey had edged away from the action.

"Not now. We have to—"

"Grant and Tino have it handled."

"But—"

"Look how happy they all are."

She was right. Cupcake was the center of an excited crowd, all of whom seemed to be trying to recite the auto mechanics' handbook. When the big dog lifted a back paw to scratch an ear, there was a general gasp and drawing back, then an embarrassed titter when he didn't spring like a panther.

I resigned myself to the inevitable. "Okay, let's go out on the deck. How did Cupcake get into the house, anyway?"

"I told him to stay outside, and he usually obeys. Someone must have bribed him with a shrimp. He'll do anything for seafood."

We settled onto a couple of Hilda's spotless canvas cushions, and I inhaled the ocean smell. "What did you want to talk about?"

"I think we should let the gang in on our investigation."

"*What?* No way. You're the only one who knows my secret, and I have no intention—"

She held up a hand, interrupting me. "We don't have to tell them about your abilities. We'll just say you're looking for your birth parents. That's true, isn't it?" She scooted closer to me on the big chaise. "I mean, you said you want to find out whether you're human. Wouldn't finding your parents settle that once and for all?"

My birth parents. It was the holy grail of my adolescence, a dream bitterly forced aside, only to be reawakened by Dominic's dark hints and half-truths.

"Say we did tell them that much. The stuff

you're looking into is hardly what someone would expect for a conventional birth parent search. How do we explain why you're looking for information about Dominic?"

"With the truth—or some of it." She put a hand on my arm, and I was proud of myself for not automatically shrugging it off. "We tell them that Dominic claimed to have information about your birth parents."

"And what if they ask the obvious question? Which is why would I believe a guy like that?"

"You did, though, didn't you? Believe him?"

I thought about it. "Not completely. But—"

"But he had abilities similar to yours, right?"

"Yes. Not as strong, at least not with the press. But he was much stronger with the telepathy. So strong he could project false visions into my mind."

"And he claimed to know who your birth parents were."

"So he said." I thought about my last conversation with Dominic. The last conversation he ever had with anyone. "He could have been lying, though."

"But you don't think so." She gave me a very direct, un-Sukey-like look. She caught my eye, and a moment of pure honesty passed between us.

"No. I don't. I was—" I took a fortifying swallow of my beer "—inside his mind. Deep inside. It was the most terrifying thing I've ever felt. He lied to me about some things. He told me you were dead, and I believed him. But no, I don't think he lied about knowing where I came from."

The harbor lights twinkled. "He wanted it so badly, Sukey. To be able to use the press as easily as I do. He had seen it before—seen someone as strong as I am. He lusted for it. That's how I was able to…"

I stopped. Even here, in this safe place, I didn't want to think about what I had done to Dominic.

Sukey's hand went down to cover my own. "You did it to save me, Mercy. To save my life. He could have told you stuff you've been wondering about since you were a little kid—given you answers. But you gave it up for me." Her eyes were welling up with tears, and I pulled my hand away before the same thing happened to me.

"So," I asked, "why do you want to tell the gang?" I straightened up and looked back out at the dark water.

"To help with the legwork." Sukey took a quick swipe at her eyes and reassumed a businesslike tone. "The information is coming in so fast, and there are about a million phone calls to make, and if any of them pan out, someone may need to go talk to someone in person. None of them has a day job, except Sam. You know how Grant is with plans and puzzles, and Tino would *love* to play detective."

I laughed. Tino had seen every mystery movie ever produced about six times and had memorized most of the dialogue. "Who do you think he'll want to be? Sherlock Holmes or James Bond?"

"Definitely Bond—better outfits." She grinned. "Does this mean I can get them to help me?"

"Yes, you can tell Grant and Tino. And Hilda— she'd just get it out of them anyway. And she always wants to drive. But not Sam."

"But Sam—"

I interrupted. "This isn't negotiable. If Sam thinks the only thing preventing me from telling him my secret is some kind of trauma over not knowing my birth parents, he'll just get all understanding and say it doesn't matter."

"Maybe it doesn't. Maybe you should just tell him."

I shook my head. "No. Not until I know…"

"If you're human," she finished for me.

I just nodded. I didn't want to say it aloud.

"All right." She stood up, apparently ready to run right in and start a group strategy session.

Excited shrieks came through the glass doors of the great room, and I scrambled to my feet. As I dashed into the house, I was greeted by applause, but it wasn't for me.

Hawaiian shirt guy lay on the floor, his neck held firmly but, apparently, without danger of strangulation by Cupcake.

"Good boy, Cupcake! You can let him up now. Come on, sit." At Grant's words, Cupcake released the man, who sat up and felt his throat gingerly. A few onlookers slapped him on the back.

"We got a new word," said Tino. "It's pi—"

Hilda slapped a hand over his mouth. "Not aloud, or he'll do it again." She released him.

"Oh, right. Sorry. It's p-i-s-t-o-n."

"As in the thing inside the cylinder?" I asked, wanting to be sure I had it right. The Official Cupcake Command List had little room for error.

"Yup," said Grant, stroking Cupcake's head. "I know you say the guy you got him from was an asshole, but he did a hell of a job training this pup. Come on, Cupcake, you just earned yourself another shrimp."

"Tino, Hilda, you got a minute?" Sukey, all eagerness, gave me a look that plainly asked if I needed to be in on the conversation.

"You go ahead, Sukey. I'm sure you can explain everything without me." Suddenly I wanted to be by myself in the open air.

"Okay. Can Cupcake bunk at my place tonight?"

"Of course. Fred could use the break." My middle-aged orange tabby hadn't been consulted about Cupcake's adoption and was still not completely sold on our new roommate.

"See you tomorrow. Oh, Grant, could you come with us, too? There's something I need to talk to you all about."

As the four of them stepped out on the deck, I dug my car keys out of my pocket and headed for the front door. Time for a good night's sleep. I had a feeling my life was going to get way too interesting, way too fast.

I wasn't wrong.

# 6

Dear Angel of Mercy,
Is Rose the freind you sent me? She is nice but to busy helping all the other peepel at the place and cant play with me. I am being good and reading books but Mommy is not geting better and it makes me sad becuase she wont read with me. Please help Mommy.
Love, Grace

"I can't tell you how incredible it was, Sukey." I listened to my own voice and felt the unfamiliar smile stretching my face. Who was this person who had taken over my body, and what had she done with me? I had just had my second session at Haven House and was going over the high points.

"This woman, Lakeesha, is twenty-one and has two children by different fathers. She was fourteen when she had the first one. Fourteen!" I took a sip of the draft beer that was making a circle of condensation on Jimbo's scarred bar. "I really, really love it."

"I can tell." Sukey was the best person to whom to tell a story—her enthusiasm didn't have to be faked. "I mean, sometimes you mention your clients, but I never see you get all excited like this."

"My clients are different. They need my help, sure. But they come in with some expectation of success or, at least, the belief that if hypnotherapy doesn't work they'll try something else. But tonight—" I struggled for the right words.

"This woman has been abused in one way or another since she can remember. She came into the session believing that's the way the world is and always will be, and she has no choice but to depend on some man, no matter how bad he is, to make sure her children are fed and there's a roof over their heads. And when she walked out…"

"And when she walked out you probably had her believing she could become the first black, former-unwed-mother president of the United States."

I laughed. "Well, no, not quite. But that she could become the kind of person her children could be proud of, anyway. And that no one—*no one*—has the right to hit her."

Sukey looked pensive, which was a switch. Generally I brooded and she gushed. "I remember when you did your press thing on me. I didn't even know you were doing it, but afterward I felt so…so *good* about myself. I couldn't imagine letting some man treat me badly ever again."

"Sukey, I've always felt a little guilty about pressing you without telling you first."

"But you do that with your clients every day."

"They're not my friends. And I know how it feels to have someone screwing around in my mind when I didn't invite them in."

"You're talking about Dominic, aren't you? He was the first person whose thoughts you heard."

"Yes, until you. I mean, I didn't even know I had the ability, and the next thing I knew, I could hear you clear as a bell."

"I think what happened to me was—"

"Your Drano theory again?" Sukey claimed that my pressing had cleaned out her psychic pipes, which was how we were able to send and receive thoughts.

"Yes. And I'm starting to wonder…have you heard anyone else's thoughts besides mine?"

"Other than Dominic's, you mean?" I shook my head. "Nope, so far it's just you."

"Well, I think I have." She looked down into

her beer. "I mean, I always thought I was a little psychic. But lately…"

I was alarmed. "When did this happen? Whose thoughts?"

She shrugged. "Oh, ever since the night we…you know."

I knew. The night she had used telepathy to lead me to the beach house where she was about to be raped and murdered.

"So far it's just little stuff. With total strangers. Like realizing the store clerk is upset because it's her lunch break and the manager hasn't come in to relieve her. Or knowing some guy in a bar is looking at my ass."

I laughed. "Some guy in a bar is *always* looking at your ass, Sukey. It's a great ass."

"Thanks." She grinned and took a sip of her beer. "But this is different. Sometimes it's creepy. I know everyone has thoughts they would rather not have anyone know about."

That was one hell of an understatement. "Nothing like that has happened to me, Sukey, but don't forget, you figured out the telepathy thing faster than I did. You were talking to me for a long time before I figured out how to talk back. I may have supplied the drain cleaner, but maybe all the water is flowing from you."

Her eyes opened very wide. "You mean *I'm* psychic and you're *not?*"

"Could be. Or I'm just a little bit psychic and you're a whole lot psychic."

"Wow!" She put down her beer, apparently too excited to drink.

"Yeah." It was nice to see someone who was actually happy about having paranormal abilities. I had always thought of mine as a curse.

"You got room for another set of elbows on this bar?"

"Hey, you made it!" I was delighted to see Rose. I had wanted to talk to her after Lakeesha's session earlier, but she had been too busy. I was pleased she had taken up my invitation to join me for a beer. "Have a seat. You remember Sukey."

She nodded and climbed onto a stool. Jimbo appeared instantly. "What can I get you?"

"A draft will be fine." Jimbo drew one from the tap but did not retreat after setting it down.

"You a friend of the Newport Bitch's?" He nodded at me.

"You kiss your mama with that mouth?" she said to him, and I almost choked on my beer.

"It's okay, Rose," I said through laughter. "Jimbo only insults people he likes." Her skeptical look only increased my amusement. "Jimbo, this is Rose. You better watch it—I'm pretty sure she can keep even you in line."

"You think so?" To my surprise, he held out his hand and Rose took it. "Nice to meet you. Even if you don't keep the best company."

Shaking his hand, Rose replied, "Nice place you got here. I like a good dive bar." She nodded toward the rack of pool cues. "Any of those sticks straighter than a corkscrew?"

Jimbo pretended to be insulted. "I don't keep bad cues in here. Players wouldn't stand for it."

"Well, maybe I'll write my name on that chalkboard and check it out myself." Rose nodded at the sign-up board used by players waiting for a turn at the single table.

"I might just play a round myself." Another surprise. Jimbo rarely played pool in his own place, and never on a busy night.

"I'll put your name up after mine. After I win the table, you can challenge me." Rose got up and went over to the chalkboard.

"Big talk." *That is one fine looking woman.*

This time I did choke on my beer. Had I just heard Jimbo's thoughts?

Sukey slapped me on the back. *I heard it, too.*

"You okay, Mercy?" Jimbo poured a short glass of tap water and placed it in front of me.

"I'm fine," I managed to croak. "Just tried to inhale some beer." When he walked away, I said, "Geeze, Sukey. You are definitely the one supplying the drain cleaner this time. You just mention hearing other people's thoughts and look what happens."

"I know." She was obviously delighted. "Maybe it was just a very strong thought. I mean, when was the last time you saw Jimbo pay any particular attention to a woman in here?"

I shook my head. "Never. But he's paying attention now."

I nodded to where Jimbo was pretending to polish glasses while keeping a careful eye on Rose, who, after writing her name on the chalkboard, was on her way back to the bar.

"I spoke with Lakeesha before I left," she said. "She's all fired up about going to community college to learn court reporting. And she didn't say a word about going back to her boyfriend. You seem to have hit the ground running, Mercy."

"I'm glad you think so." I signaled Jimbo for a refill. "When I look around the shelter, I think about how those women could be the girls I grew up with when I was a ward of the state."

"You were in foster care in California?" Rose took a pull on her draft, and I sensed Sukey sidling in a bit closer. She knew part of the story, but no one had ever heard it all.

"New Jersey. But I don't think it was much different."

Sukey chimed in. "I've been meaning to get the details so I can start my Internet search. I know you never knew your birth parents. Do you know *anything* about them?"

"Nothing. I was abandoned at birth. At least that's what my adoptive parents told me."

"Where are they now? Your adoptive parents, I mean."

"I have no idea. They gave me up to the state when I was eleven. After that I was in foster homes."

"Oh, *Mercy!*" Sukey was the youngest of seven siblings, and at thirty still called her parents Mommy and Daddy. It was a close family, and she talked to all of them two or three times a week, and although they had scattered around the world as adults, they visited one another frequently. I had attended a family gathering with her once, and had found their effortless, noisy camaraderie both attractive and terrifying.

"I'm so sorry." She reached across the bar and took my hand. I automatically pulled it away, then winced when I noticed the flicker of hurt that ran across her features. I checked out Rose's face to see what she thought about this little drama, but she had suddenly become very interested in the decorations behind the bar.

"At any rate, I'm glad it went well with Chantal and Lakeesha, and I plan to be back next week."

Rose fidgeted with a bar napkin. "Actually, I was wondering if you might be able to free up a little time before that. Kind of an emergency case."

I frowned. "Well, my office is usually pretty crazy on Saturday. What did you have in mind?"

She looked uncharacteristically reticent. "If you don't mind, I prefer to talk about it in private. There's a confidentiality issue."

"Do you want me to go?" Sukey started to pick up her beer.

"No, no, you sit. I'm going to relax and play a little pool first. Then Mercy and I can have a talk."

"Hey, mama." Tino slid onto a stool on Sukey's right and nodded at me. Hilda hovered behind him.

"Tino, that's the only seat," she said, and puzzlement flitted over Tino's face before he realized his error and sprang to his feet.

"You take it," he offered with a flourish, as if he hadn't required a reminder to be gallant.

Hilda perched on the stool as if the seedy bar had been transported to the Ritz Carlton. "Club soda, please," she told Jimbo. "And Tino wants a Jack and Coke."

"Is that you, Mrs. Bennington?" Rose got to her feet and came around to take Hilda's hand. "I'm Rosalee Jackson. I never got to thank you for your donation. We've done great things with it. You should stop by and see."

Hilda basked in the glow of largesse appreciated. "So nice to see you, Ms. Jackson. What brings you to our local haunts?"

"Mercy is doing some volunteer work at Haven House. And call me Rose." As the two of them chatted, I saw another familiar figure in the doorway.

"Hey, Grant. Feeling any older?"

"Nah, I'm planning to live to be a hundred and fifty. Another year isn't going to make much of a difference." He saw me scanning the doorway behind him and guessed the reason. "Sam's boat wasn't at the dock."

"Oh. Oh, right, he did mention going sailing." *But I didn't think he would go without me.*

"Sukey told me about your quest."

My heart actually skipped a beat. "My… quest?"

"For your birth parents," he supplied. Relief made me glad I was already sitting down. "She said Dominic said he knew them."

"Dominic said a lot of things. Not all of them true."

"But you believed this one."

"Yeah."

Grant gave me a sharp look but must have decided to accept my statement without asking for a reason. "All right. I told Sukey we need to sketch out a plan."

"You and your plans." I felt myself grinning. My mood had been too good for regrets over Sam and worry about my secret becoming known to squelch it entirely. "Do you have a diagram for everything?"

"Doesn't everyone?" He feigned surprise, and I laughed outright.

"I got one." Tino had apparently grown tired of Rose and Hilda's chitchat. "I'm diagramming how to kick your ass if you make me study any more of that chemistry shit." Tino shook his head in disgust. "That periodic table's gonna make my head explode."

"It's just memorization, Tino. You have an excellent memory when you want to." Grant turned to me. "And he's going to blow the math tests away. He's a walking calculator."

"The reading comprehension's the bitch, though." Tino drained his cocktail. "I guess I shoulda read more books."

Grant clapped him on the shoulder. "You have the rest of your life for that, my boy. And I have a house full of books. You ever hear of Walter Mosely?"

"He a writer?" Tino looked genuinely interested.

My beer finished, I slid from my barstool and headed for the women's room to relieve my full bladder. As I washed my hands, I scanned the walls for words of wisdom. Jimbo's had received an honorable mention in a national magazine in the Best Bathroom Graffiti category, according to a framed article on the wall near the pool table. Most of the scrawls were familiar, but I finally spotted something new.

In one handwriting: *My husband follows me everywhere.*

In another: *I do not!*

When I returned to the barroom, Rose was playing pool against Lifeguard Skip and, to the delight of the regulars, winning. Skip was a better-than-average player and arrogant about it. I watched as Rose, having no shot of her own, used her turn to nestle the cue ball into a spot that would require Skip to break out of a logjam to try for his one unlikely shot, a move that would only improve her position. The look on Skip's face was priceless.

I returned to the bar, where Jimbo was watching the action with great interest. "You're going to have your work cut out for you, Jimbo."

"You ain't kidding." I wondered if he was talking about more than the pool game.

"What I'm about to tell you has to remain in strictest confidence." I couldn't see Rose's face very well. A palm tree blocked the overhead light. We had left Jimbo's and headed north along the bay front, away from the glare and noise of the Fun Zone, and now sat on a sidewalk bench in front of a house where no interior lights shone.

"What is it?" Rose's caution had kindled my curiosity. "I know everything at Haven House has to remain confidential."

She shook her head. "This isn't about Haven House." She looked up, and I caught a glimpse of her expression. She looked grim.

"Sometimes there are cases where women need to hide a little deeper than Haven House. We aren't easy to find, but it can be done. We get state funding—precious little, but some. And where there's a paper trail, there's a way to track it."

"You mean abusers have found Haven House in the past?" I was alarmed. Chantal had described the man who had broken her ribs and given her several concussions as "big enough to play pro football, except he always fails the drug test."

"Not often, but yeah." She inhaled deeply, then sighed. "If they have the resources. Police connections, or money to hire investigators."

"I wouldn't think an abuser would want to get some friend in the police department to help him find an abused spouse."

"Not all connections to the police department are friendly. Some are strictly monetary. There was this one guy, drug supplier or something, already had some cops on his payroll."

I got the picture.

"So how do you hide them...deeper?"

"There are places." She sat up straighter, getting down to business. "Off the books. Not associated with Haven House or me or anyone whose name could be traced back to the system. We could lose our licenses if anyone ever found out."

"Sounds complicated."

"It is." She stood up and stretched. "We have

to do things in cash, and cash is one thing that's pretty hard to come by in my line of work. But it's essential for two reasons. One, there can't be any trail for the abusers to trace. And two…" She trailed off.

"And two?"

"Well, it's illegal. At least part of the time. There are women who don't have legal custody of their children, even though they should, so they're kidnappers under the law. Their husbands have the legal resources or political influence to take the kids away. Or, even worse, the husbands have connections to organized crime."

A shiver ran through me. "Scary shit."

"You are right about that, sister."

I let that sink in, then made up my mind. "How do you need me to help?"

She laughed softly and sat back down. "You surprise me, Mercy. You come off all prickly, then when someone needs help you turn into butter and flat out offer."

*Butter? Me?* I shook my head. "It's why we went for a walk, that's all. You were going to ask me to do something for you."

"Not for me. For Anna and Grace. Or at least for Anna."

"Who are they?"

"Some very badly damaged people. I don't even know everything that has been done to Anna. She's so messed up she can't even look me in the face or make a whole sentence without falling apart. She cries so much you'd think she was gonna dry up and blow away."

I felt a lump of something beginning to form in the pit of my stomach. Anger, I realized, at anyone who could make a woman so fragile she couldn't speak to someone as understanding as Rosalee Jackson.

"And Grace is the most beautiful child you have ever seen. About six, and looks like a fairy princess. But her eyes are a hundred years old. She doesn't talk at all, at least not to me. But Anna says she's unusually bright, and she writes all the time in this diary. I haven't seen most of what she puts down—she's got a death grip on that book. But I caught a couple of glimpses, and it sure doesn't look like the work of a six-year-old to me."

"You want me to hypnotize them?"

"Just Anna, for now. You have any experience working with children?"

"No."

"Well, I would prefer you didn't make someone quite this damaged your first subject."

I felt a flash of annoyance but didn't argue. She was right. I didn't really know how the press would affect a six-year-old.

"No one has been able to get Anna to open up, and she seems to be getting worse, not better. And I'm afraid we'll run out of time."

"Why?"

"Phil—that's her husband—is one of the few men who found the address of Haven House. He showed up there looking for them."

"What? Is that why you moved them?"

"I already had. Anna had kept saying he would find her—that he knew people everywhere and someone would give him the address. A lot of the women are paranoid, but I believed her. And it's a good thing I did."

"No shit."

"Normally I would believe there's no way he could use his connections to find the safe house where I have them now. But when I told Anna that Phil had come to Haven House looking for them, she freaked out. However uncommunicative she had been before, it got worse. She shut down completely."

"So you want me to get her to talk?" I could do that.

"Yes, for starters. I would prefer you didn't

make a lot of post-hypnotic suggestions or instructions until we find out what the damage is. What she's been through."

I didn't like the idea of compelling Anna to show me her pain and then stopping without doing anything to ease it. Rose must have seen my frown, because she said, "You got a problem with that?"

"Yeah, a little. I understand we need to have a strategy before I decide what to tell—before I decide on a course of treatment. But couldn't I at least give her a little comfort?"

"Like how?"

I had to be careful. Rose was too smart not to smell an outright lie, even from a world-champion liar like me. "Well, sometimes during a hypnotic trance, I can tell someone that they feel relaxed or safe. It usually works."

She digested that. "Okay, you can tell her there are people who care about her, and that we'll do everything we can to keep her safe. That much is true."

"And that she can feel better about herself," I added. When Rose didn't immediately agree, I went on. "Assuming, of course, she has self-esteem issues. Which seems likely."

Rose sighed. "Yeah, it's probably a safe bet. Go

ahead and tell her that. Maybe it will make her stop crying twenty-four hours a day."

"What about Grace?" I asked, thinking about the fairy princess with centenarian eyes.

"No, not yet." Rose was firm. "But you can ask Anna to tell you what she knows. If Phil has hurt the girl, or what that child has seen."

I shivered. As we walked back toward the lights and music of the Fun Zone, the words echoed in my head. *What that child has seen.*

# 7

Dear Angel of Mercy,
Mommy is very sad agian today and I am worrided about her. I no you can make her have good dreams and she will feel better and can read a book to me and we can bake cookies and go to the park. I dont no if there is a park heer. But you can make a park with flowers. Mommy loves flowers and I like them to.
Love, Grace

Although Saturday was a busy day at my office, I gave myself the indulgence of starting my business hours at ten. Hey, if I liked to have a few beers on Friday night, so did my clients, right? At least that was my reasoning.

So when I woke up with an orange cat approximately two centimeters from my face, I wasn't thrilled to see 6:15 glowing from my digital clock.

"Fred, it's not even daylight," I mumbled, turning over to put my head under the pillow. Within seconds a persistent paw reached beneath and touched the end of my nose.

"Me*ow!*" Fred pronounced it like it was spelled, with the accent on the second syllable. Clearly cat-speak for "I'm up. Why aren't you?" I surrendered to the inevitable and emerged from under my shelter to muss the striped head.

"Kind of nice not to have some big dog panting all over us, huh?" Fred purred his agreement. Cupcake had spent another night with Sukey.

I was out of coffee, a major catastrophe, so after getting dressed, I decided to leave early and treat myself to breakfast at Charlie's Chili before work. I was just trying to choose between the sourdough French toast and the signature chili cheese omelet when the bell over the door jingled and Sukey walked in.

"I thought I recognized your car." She slid into the booth opposite and signaled the waiter for coffee. "You order yet?"

I shook my head. "Where's Cupcake?" I squinted to peer out the plate-glass window.

"Tied to a parking meter." I must have looked alarmed, because she continued. "Don't worry, he won't attack anyone."

"Not unless they say the wrong thing." I watched as the waiter put down a cup for Sukey and filled it, then topped off mine. Sukey ordered the omelet, and I went for the French toast. The doorbell jingled again, and Grant appeared.

"I don't know why I'm surprised to see you," I said, as he sat next to Sukey. "Once you get started on something, you're like a brushfire in a canyon."

"No time like the present," he said, craning his neck to find the waiter. "Carlos, get me the usual, okay?"

"Sure thing."

"I eat breakfast here more than I do at home," he said by way of explanation. "Sukey, did you bring the papers you told me about?"

"Here." Sukey reached into her voluminous bag and pulled out the now-familiar folder full of information on Rocko. "I marked the pages we were discussing."

Grant drew out a pair of black-rimmed reading glasses and perused the files. "I see what you mean. He's been on parole twice."

"Yeah," said Sukey. "That should be really helpful."

"Why is that?" I was definitely playing catch-up here.

"Because he would have told his parole officer if he was working. And if he had a job, he had coworkers. And if he had coworkers—"

"He may have made friends with some of them," finished Grant. "A few beers, and they're trading war stories. 'My childhood was worse than your childhood.'"

"Oh, yeah, Rocko's a touchy-feely kind of guy." I heard the acid in my tone at the same time I saw Grant wince. "Sorry, Grant, but I just can't see Rocko sitting around telling everyone how his big, bad foster daddy mistreated him."

"You never know," said Sukey. "He likes to talk about himself. And he loves to brag about all the fights he's been in. Maybe he beat up his foster parents. Maybe Dominic helped."

I shrugged, still skeptical.

Grant cleared his throat. "Mercy, I think Sukey has a pretty damned good idea here. Career criminals like Rocko start young. He knew Dominic when he was a child and was still in touch with him as an adult." He sipped his coffee. "And Dominic was the boss—the dynamic of that relationship probably started when they were still kids. If Rocko had buddies, there's a damned good chance he talked about Dominic. Some of them may even have met him."

I felt chastised and didn't like it. It was a good thing the food arrived, or I probably would have made another sarcastic comment. When cornered, I stick with my strengths.

"Trade you half an omelet for some of that French toast." If Sukey's feelings were hurt by my doubts, her tone wasn't conveying it. I pushed my plate forward, and we made the transfer.

One bite of the gooey omelet and I felt less cranky. I took a deep breath and tried out this apology thing. "Sorry, Sukey. Grant is right. It's a really good line of investigation."

I had used the "investigation" word on purpose, and it must have struck the right note, because she beamed. "Thanks, Mercy. And I have some others. Look here." She reopened her folder and took out what looked like a partially completed form. As she swung it around to face me, I saw it was a pho-tocopied page from *The Exciting World of Private Investigation* with the header Explore Every Avenue. There was a section entitled Public Records, and another called Confidential Files. Sukey had filled in the blanks with notes about arrests, foster care, parole, employment and apart-ment rentals.

"Wow." I was dazed. "Do you really have all this stuff?"

She shook her head. "No, like it says, some of it is confidential, so you have to find a source."

"Like a parole officer?" I was getting interested in spite of myself.

"Yeah, or like Detective Gerson's cousin at Family Services. Also, some of this stuff is guesses—see the question marks? Rocko mentioned some places he lived, so I thought I would start calling up apartment complexes and stuff. I might get lucky."

"You are a force to be reckoned with, Sukey." Grant wiped his lips with a napkin. "And I'll help with the phone calls, or with driving out to talk to people in person."

"Okay, Grant, but if we get to question someone, I'm coming along." Sukey tapped her notes. "I didn't do all this work just to miss my very first interrogation. Although—" she grinned, blushing "—I haven't finished reading that chapter yet."

What I had started thinking of as the "underground shelter" was actually an over-the-garage apartment that faced an alley on Balboa Island. The owner of the corresponding house, which faced the street, was a retired dentist who was seldom in residence. Rose had explained that he had given her the keys to the mother-in-law with the caveat that he really didn't need to know who was staying there, but he didn't want any calls from his neighbors complaining about noisy kids or junk cars parked in the alley. When you live in a neighborhood where the homes are less than twelve feet apart, you have to respect one another's space.

I would have thought this location too visible, even though at first glance it appeared to be unoccupied. The blinds were tightly drawn, and the flower boxes along the tiny balcony were empty, devoid even of weeds. But Rose's knock had been answered so quickly that I knew Anna must have been peeking out, anxiously awaiting our arrival. In fact, Anna looked as if anxious was her normal state.

"Where's Grace?" asked Rose, after making introductions.

"In the back." Anna's voice was whisper-quiet and would have been virtually impossible to hear if the apartment itself had not been so silent. Her eyes, too restless to settle on anything for long, flicked toward a closed door that must have led to a bedroom. I thought it was too quiet for a six-year-old child to be behind it, but Rose nodded.

"I'll sit with her while you two talk," she said,

and Anna lifted her head long enough for me to see a flash of panic in her eyes. Clearly she was terrified of being left alone with a stranger. I tasted her fear in my own throat, acrid and stinging.

"We'll be fine. Won't we, Anna?" I didn't have her full attention, so I couldn't press her yet, and I wanted to at least tell her not to be afraid of me. "Do you have something I could drink, ice water maybe?"

"I have tea." Still not looking at me, she eased past me around the corner of the kitchen counter and went to the refrigerator. The act of filling a glass with ice and tea calmed her a little, or at least I thought so until I noticed her hand shaking as she handed it to me.

"Aren't you going to have some?" She shook her head. I looked around at the simple furnishings and settled onto a threadbare love seat. The sofa was directly opposite in the narrow room, but she still stood as if ready to flee. I had a feeling the child in the other room was the only thing stopping her. "Sit down, Anna. You don't have to be afraid of me." My press felt like a blind shot, and her mind a target that skittered and danced in my sights, but I must have caught a corner of something, because she sank onto the sofa.

"Look at me, please. I won't harm you." This

time she was paying full attention, and her eyes finally ceased their restless ballet and focused on mine. And what eyes! I felt a tightness in my chest and realized I was holding my breath. Her apprehension was contagious, and I would have to calm myself first if I was to be of any use to her. I took a moment to study my subject.

She was painfully thin, with lank brown hair that fell around her face but failed to conceal the shadows made by sharp cheekbones and a pointed chin. The hollows under her eyes looked like bruises against her pale skin, and her dark eyes seemed enormous. I had seen eyes like that in photographs of war refugees and survivors of natural disasters. Small boned, she would have been petite in any case. Now she looked as if a strong wind would send her blowing down the road like a tumbleweed.

Well, maybe I could do something about that. I knew today's mission was supposed to be fact-finding only, but there was no way I could look into Anna's eyes and not try to drain the endless wells of sorrow I saw there. Wondering if Rose was listening through the door, I started.

"Anna, I want you to take a deep breath and let it out. I want you to feel yourself relax. You can feel safe here today. Do you feel safe?"

"Y-yes." The response was barely audible, but I saw some of the tension leave her shoulders. I hadn't noticed that her hands were balled into fists until she unclenched them.

"Very good, Anna." My subjects didn't really require reinforcement, but I was unable to resist this small show of kindness. She looked like she needed it. "Anna, I want you to tell me how you are taking care of yourself. Are you eating regular meals?" This was off the script, and I half expected Rose to barge in and ask what the hell I was doing, but she didn't. I thought I could hear her voice droning from the bedroom, as if she were reading to the child.

"No," said Anna in response to my question. Then she added, "I'm not hungry." I was surprised, because I hadn't asked, "why not?" Sometimes my clients volunteered information during sessions without being pressed to do so, but not often. Anna must be especially susceptible to the press. Which was good, wasn't it? A sour note of unease threatened to rise from my subconscious, but I moved on.

"Anna, it is important that you eat healthy meals on a regular basis. Do you prepare meals for Grace?"

"Yes."

"From now on, when you make a meal for Grace, you will make enough for both of you, and you will eat, too. Will you do that?"

She frowned, but said, "Okay."

"Very good. You're doing great, Anna." Again I felt that need to reassure. "Are you able to sleep?"

"No."

It was the answer I expected, but I wasn't really sure how to respond. Could I simply order someone not to have insomnia? What if the reasons were physiological? I doubted that was the case. Also, I had to be careful—the way Anna responded, I might put her into a coma if I didn't watch it. I considered my phrasing.

"When it is time for you to sleep, you will be able to relax. You will be able to…to set aside any thoughts that are causing you anxiety and preventing you from falling asleep." I paused, unwilling to say more on the subject. I thought what I had said so far was safe, and I hoped it would be enough. "Do you understand?"

"Yes."

I took a deep breath. It was time to get down to the real business of the session.

"Anna, I want you to tell me about your husband."

She stiffened, but spoke. "His name is Phil. Phillip Green." Her brow creased, and I understood she needed more prompting. Rose and I had spoken about this, and she had suggested I ask about the relationship in general before getting into the specifics of the abuse.

"Tell me about when and how you met him, and how you ended up married to him."

She was quiet for a moment, but I sensed no resistance. It was like she was putting her thoughts in order. "I was a waitress at the Dolphin Café. He came to breakfast almost every day. He said I was pretty."

Her eyes changed. It was spooky—one minute I was looking into black pools of despair, and the next moment I saw normal brown eyes. I could almost see the young woman who had worked at the lively diner on a side street off the boardwalk that had closed up a few years back. Almost.

"No one ever said I was pretty before. He always sat in my section. He asked me to go to a movie with him. I said yes." I felt the hairs on my arm stand up as her voice morphed from the tortured whisper to a normal, if soft, speaking voice. Nothing like this had ever happened in any sessions with my other clients. I was watching Anna turn into the person she had been before she married Phil.

"We went on a few dates, and he told me I should marry him. So I did." She stopped, having fulfilled my instruction.

"Phil told you should marry him? He didn't ask you?" Her choice of words had puzzled me.

"He said no one else would want me, because I was so stupid and because I was frigid in bed." The voice began to morph back the other way, with a strained tone creeping in. Turning into the voice of the woman Phil had started to mold into the frightened creature who had answered the door.

"Anna, you're not stupid. And you're not—" I glanced toward the bedroom door, catching myself. I had been about to tell her she wasn't frigid but had realized in time I was overstepping the bounds of this session. Anna's sexual problems, real or imagined by Phil, could be dealt with later. I had another agenda tonight.

I took a deep breath to calm myself. "Anna, tell me about what it was like when you and Phil were first married."

Again that pause as she put her thoughts together. "Phil said I should quit my job, so I did. He bought a house, and we moved in. I went with him to pick out furniture and things for the house, and it was fun fixing it up." Some of the strain left her voice, and her eyes got a faraway look, then darkened again almost immediately. "But after the house was done, Phil didn't want me to go anywhere. He wouldn't let me drive, and he got mad when I walked to the store. He said I had to stay in the house."

She stopped again, and I prompted, "What happened when Phil got mad?"

"He hit me." I waited for more, but it didn't come.

"How did he hit you? How many times?" I struggled to keep my voice even.

"He slapped me and punched me. I had a black eye afterward, and my lip was bleeding." Her voice tightened further. "It hurt."

I had to work to keep my breathing under control. "Tell me about when Phil hurt you after that first time. How often, and how badly?"

"Not very often at first. Once or twice a month, and he mostly slapped me. Sometimes I would have some bruises or…or some broken skin. Then…" Her voice was now back to the almost-whisper I had heard when I arrived. "Then it started happening more often. At least once a week. And he started punching and kicking. Sometimes I had to go to the hospital."

"Did you think about leaving him?" Rose had

said to be very careful about this topic at this early stage, but I wanted to know.

"Yes. But I couldn't."

"Why did you feel like you couldn't leave?"

"Because he would find me. He told me he would always be able to find me. Phil is very smart, and he knows a lot of important people."

"I see." I didn't, not really. I had read and seen enough to know that many abused women felt trapped, and some of them really were. But I believed there was always a way to get out.

And Anna *had* gotten out, I reminded myself. Somehow she had found her way into Rose's care. For herself, and for the little girl, Grace.

I glanced at the clock. I wanted to keep this first session short, because I was navigating unfamiliar waters and needed to stay sharp. The things Anna was telling me were making me angry, and I'm most likely to lose control of the press when I'm upset.

I had two goals for this session—three, if I counted spending a little time making Anna feel better about herself. I needed to find out the extent of the abuse, which I already had, even if only in general terms. And I needed to find out whether Grace had seen it or been harmed herself. Time to move on to this topic.

"How long were you and Phil married when Grace was born?"

"A year."

"How did Phil feel about the pregnancy?"

"He said he was happy." Anna's voice trembled. "He didn't hit me as much once I got big. But as soon as she was born he started in again, worse than before."

I gritted my teeth. Now was not the time to lose my temper. "And how did he act around Grace?"

"At first he got mad because she wasn't a boy, and because she cried all the time. He went out at night a lot and didn't come back until the next day."

"And as she got older?"

"He didn't pay any attention to her at all. It was like she didn't exist for him. Until she turned five."

A weird tickle started at the back of my neck. "Anna, tell me what happened when Grace turned five. How did Phil's behavior change toward her?"

"It was like he noticed her for the first time. He played with her and talked to her all the time. He started bringing her presents. Dolls and clothes, lots of clothes. Really fancy dresses. He called her his princess."

It all sounded harmless enough, but Anna's whole posture had tightened until she looked like a spring that was wound too tightly. Something about Phil's sudden interest in his child had obviously made her very uncomfortable.

"Did Grace enjoy the attention?"

"At first."

"But that changed?"

"Yes."

I looked at Anna's rigid shoulders and stole another glance at the clock. "Anna, I'm almost done asking you questions. I know it's hard to talk about these things, but you can trust me, and you can feel better because you are telling me. I want you to imagine that while you are letting the story out, you are also letting the stress and tension out. You will feel more relaxed. Do you feel more relaxed?"

"Yes," she replied, and I watched her shoulders lower to a more natural position. I realized my own posture was almost as tense as hers, and I took a couple of deep breaths.

"Anna, you said that Grace's attitude toward her father changed. How did it change, and what was happening when the change took place? Remember, as you tell me, the pressure you have been under while you have been keeping this to yourself will continue to lessen."

When she spoke, her voice was almost back to

the normal tones she had used when describing her life at the time she met Phil. "Grace loved spending time with her daddy. It was like they were in a club. I wasn't a member. Phil started taking Grace out with him in the car. They went shopping and went to restaurants. They whispered and giggled together all the time. It was like they were…dating."

At the word "dating" I felt something clench deep in my abdomen. I almost told Anna to stop, to give me a moment to catch my breath before she went on. But the command I had given her was still in effect, and her oddly serene voice continued.

"Then, after about a year, the giggling stopped, and Grace started to get quiet. She almost stopped talking altogether. Phil took her out less during the day and more in the evenings. Then one night they stayed out all night."

She stopped, and it was time for me to ask another question, but my vocal cords felt paralyzed. Finally I managed to croak, "Did you ask Grace where they had been?"

"Yes."

"And what did she say?" My voice sounded strange to my own ears.

"She said it was a secret. That Daddy told her she was not allowed to tell me."

"And did—" I struggled to continue "—did you let it go at that?"

"No. I kept after her, and she finally told me she went with Daddy to see his friends. But when I asked her about the friends—who they were and what they were doing—she closed her mouth and didn't say another word. She didn't say anything for over a day."

*Oh, hell. Please don't let this be what it sounds like.* "And…and did Phil take her away overnight again?"

"Yes. Four more times."

I swallowed, trying to swallow the fist-size lump that had suddenly filled my throat. "Did you ever ask Phil where he was taking her?"

"Yes."

"What did he tell you?"

"That it was none of my business. He said I was too stupid to understand, and it was my fault anyway."

"Your fault?"

"For being frigid."

My heart rate must have been at least one hundred and fifty. "Then what happened?"

"He broke my nose. And then he got in his car and drove away. And then…" She swiveled her head around and turned those empty eyes directly at me. "I took Grace and I walked to the super-market. I got a phone book and I looked up women's shelters, and I called Haven House. Ms. Jackson came and got us."

The eyes bored into me, although her tone remained perfectly calm. "Rose moved us over here after a few days. But I know Phil will find us. He'll never let us get away. He already found Haven House. He'll keep looking and looking, and he'll get his friends to help. He'll kill me, and then he'll take Grace. He'll take her, and no one will be able to stop him."

I felt like I had run a marathon, but I pushed on. "Anna, did you ever find out what Phil and his friends did to Grace? Did she ever tell you?"

"No," she said simply. "No, she won't tell me. She won't tell anyone. No one can get her to talk."

*I wouldn't bet on that.*

# 8

Dear Angel of Mercy,
Sometimes I miss Daddy but then I remeber the bad things. There is nothing to do at this new place. Maybe I can have a kitty. If I had a kitty I woodunt be lonley. Mommy is not as sad today. Did you make her have good dreams?
Love, Grace

"Mercy, are you listening to me?"

Sukey's voice made me jump. I realized I hadn't heard a word she'd said in...how many minutes? Five? Ten?

"I'm sorry. You were talking about Rocko's... what?"

She sat down on the wicker sofa that filled most of one end of my patio. "You're thinking about that little girl, aren't you?"

I hadn't told Sukey the whole story of Anna's

session, but I had let her know that I'd gone to counsel a battered woman and had learned enough to be pretty certain her daughter had been sexually abused, as well. She knew I was frustrated because I wanted to talk to Grace—to verify or discount what I most feared—and Rose had nixed the idea.

"You said yourself you don't have any experience with children, Mercy," Rose had said between sips of a milkshake at Ruby's, the diner at the end of the Balboa pier. After leaving Anna, we had crossed on the Balboa Island ferry and walked while I told Rose what I had learned. While she agreed that it sounded like Grace might have been the victim of incest, she was reluctant to call the police until we had confirmation. That was fine with me, except she wouldn't let me talk to Grace to confirm it.

"If Grace *has* been sexually abused, she's going to need help from a specialist. I'm going to get in touch with some people I know and see if I can get someone to go over there and interview her."

"But I could give it a try first. We might find out something concrete, and then we could get the legal process started."

"It's not likely you'd learn anything in one session," she countered, shaking her head. "It often takes weeks of therapy to get a child to tell the story."

*Not if I'm the one doing the therapy,* I almost said. The temptation to press Rose and convince her to take me back to the apartment was almost overwhelming. But I don't press friends without their permission—it's one of my rules. Almost never, anyway. I had broken way too many of my own rules during the Dominic incident, and I didn't want to head back down that road.

Rose must have taken my silence for surrender, because she went on, "You know, Grace said something funny to me today, which is unusual, because, as far as I know, she hasn't spoken to anyone in weeks."

"What's that?"

"Well, when I called in to see if you were finished, I must have used your first name."

"You did. Why?"

"Because she asked me, 'Is the angel of mercy here?'"

I snorted. "I have definitely never been mistaken for an angel."

She grinned and said, "Yeah, I didn't figure it for one of your nicknames. But she was so serious when she asked me. And for once her face had a real expression on it. She looked…I don't know.

Expectant. Or hopeful." Rose shook her head. "I see a lot with my job, but this one really gets to me. She's so fragile, like a little bird."

I hadn't even really seen her—just a glimpse of blond hair and huge eyes through a crack in the bedroom door as Rose came back out to the apartment's main room. But now, as I sat in the dusk, listening to the waves I couldn't quite see, she was on my mind.

"Do you want me to go home?" asked Sukey. "I can bring this stuff by tomorrow. Or we can go over it at the office on Monday."

I sighed. "No, go ahead and show it to me now. It'll take my mind off the other thing."

"We've already covered most of it. I was just telling you that although I haven't seen any of Rocko's juvenile-court records yet, I did get this." She handed me a copy of a legal-looking form entitled Release of Minor.

"Clarence Rockford Peretti," I read aloud. "Rocko's real first name is *Clarence?*"

"Yeah, he must have had it legally changed. Later records just say 'Rockford.' This is the document that officially released him from foster care when he turned eighteen."

I looked at the lengthy form, which seemed filled with minutiae. "Why is this important?"

"See the signature at the bottom? The one on the right?"

I squinted and found what she was talking about. A name was typed in a box entitled Caseworker at Time of Release, and the corresponding signature was below.

"It says Katherine Barrons." I handed the paper back to Sukey.

"Exactly," she said. "If she was his caseworker for a long time, she may know something about the foster homes he was in. She may even have been Dominic's caseworker."

I resisted the urge to grin at her excited expression. "Does she still work for the state?"

The light in Sukey's eyes dimmed slightly. "No, I called, and she retired a few years back. But I did an Internet search, and I think I found her in a retirement community out near Riverside. The property records show the house was purchased about the right time. I couldn't find a phone number, but I'm going to try to drive out there tomorrow."

"Maybe I'll come with you," I said, not really wanting to, but feeling a little guilty that she was doing all this work on my behalf.

"If you want. But Grant and Hilda both offered, too. You really don't need to get directly involved

unless we find someone who might have real information. Especially if they need a little encour-
agement to pass it on."

"Sukey, I'm not going to press someone to
make them talk to me." Visions of B-movie interrogation chambers danced in my head. *Vee haff
vays of making you talk.*

"Well, maybe you could just make them feel a
little more relaxed, so they'd spill on their own.
That wouldn't be against your ethics, would it?"

"I'd have to think about it." When I had formulated my personal rules about using the press, I'd
thought they were pretty black and white. I didn't
like blurring the edges. "And anyway, I should
probably be paying you for this, but I can't really
afford it right now."

She waved a hand dismissively. "It's good
practice for me. You could let me use your gas card
if you want, but if Hilda's driving, it doesn't matter.
She'd be insulted if you tried to give her money."

"Let me get it for you. I almost never use it." I
found the card and handed it over.

"Thanks," she said, slipping it into her suitcase-
size purse.

"No problem." I registered what she'd said
earlier. "What do you mean by 'good practice'?
What are you practicing for?"

"Oh, you never know," she said mysteriously. "Running your office is hardly a full-time job, especially now that I've got everything automated. I may want to branch out sometime in the future."

"Susan Keystone, private eye?" I smiled at the image. It really wasn't as far-fetched as my tone conveyed.

"Hmmm." She tilted her head, as if considering the idea for the first time—which I could see was not the case. "Listen, there's something else we need to talk about." She seemed a little nervous.

"What's that?"

"Your adoption records. We need to get them."

"My adoption records?" I don't know why I was surprised; it was such an obvious avenue of investigation. I just so seldom thought about my adoptive parents. I had tried calling them a few times when life at various foster and group homes got especially rough. After a couple of unsatisfactory conversations, the phone number had been disconnected. When, years later, I had passed by the house where I'd last lived with them, another family was living there. "I don't know how to go about getting them. Do you?"

"Maybe. There are a few organizations that help birth families find one another, and they have a lot of information. It varies a lot by state. Where was your adoption?"

I thought about it. "I'm not entirely sure. Rhode Island, maybe. Or Massachusetts. We moved around a lot while I was really small. The first place I remember clearly was in New Jersey, but I don't think we had lived there very long. I vaguely remember my father—my adoptive father—talking about having a job in Providence."

"Well, we'll have to find them. Your adoptive parents, I mean. They may still have the records, and even if they don't, they'll be able to tell us where they went to court."

A bitter taste filled my mouth at the thought of seeing the people who had such a tenuous connection with their adopted daughter that they had given up at the first sign of trouble. Okay, it was pretty serious trouble, but good parents don't just walk away when the going gets tough.

"I really don't want to talk to them," I told Sukey. "Not if there's any way we can get the information without them."

"*You* don't have to talk to them. Or at least I hope not—I don't blame you for not wanting to see them. But you at least have to tell me their names, and the last address you remember."

"Roberta and Thomas. She goes by Bobbie." I

hadn't said the names aloud in years, and it did nothing to improve the sourness in the back of my mouth.

"Hollings? You kept the name?" Sukey had pulled out a notepad and was taking down the information.

"Yeah." At first I'd thought someone might adopt me and change it. By the time I realized that wasn't going to happen, it hadn't seemed worth the trouble.

"And an address?"

I recited a street address in Newark. "I think they may have changed the street numbers since then—I remember that from when I went back. But it shouldn't be too hard to find the right house."

Sukey nodded, and put the pad and pen back in her purse. "Thanks, Mercy. I know it can't be easy thinking about this stuff."

"It's okay. After this morning, my own childhood family problems seem pretty tame."

"Yeah." She got up and headed toward the gate to the boardwalk. "Look, Mercy, don't make yourself crazy over that little girl, okay? Rose seems like she would be really good at taking care of things, and if she needs your help, she'll definitely ask for it."

"I hope so." But after our conversation this afternoon, I wasn't at all confident it would happen.

After Sukey left, I sat on the patio for a long time. California nights are cool, and by the time I retreated into the house I was chilled, so I hit the switch that turned on my gas fireplace.

I thought about my adoptive parents. Tom and Bobbie hadn't been the Cleavers, but neither had they been abusive. While I didn't remember feeling deeply loved, I had felt safe in their—our—home. Bobbie had gone through the motions, packing lunches and asking about homework. Tom had taught me how to throw a softball and driven me to swimming lessons at the public pool on Saturday mornings, and sometimes we all got in the car together and went to a movie, or to church on Sunday.

*Church.* Who had just been talking about church recently? It was Rose—she had mentioned singing in her church choir when we had lunch the other day. *So she'll be busy tomorrow morning.* The thought flitted across my consciousness like a whisper.

I actually scolded myself aloud. "No, Mercy, you will not go over there tomorrow morning. Rose asked you to stay away, and you have to respect that."

*But Rose doesn't have to know. I can instruct*

*Grace and Anna not to tell her. They won't even remember my visit, if I don't want them to.*

I was tired, I realized. And it was making me mentally weak. What I needed was a good night's sleep.

"Woof." Cupcake's big head eased into my lap, and he gave me an expressive look.

"Need a little walk before bedtime, pup?" I asked, and he wagged his stump of a tail enthusiastically, thumping it loudly against the side of a chair.

"Okay, let's do it." He obligingly retrieved his leash, and I took him down to the edge of the water.

Newport Beach prohibits dogs on the beach, but they relax this restriction in the off-season, during evening and early morning hours. By the time the big rottweiler had raced back and forth along the water's edge a half-dozen times, making me laugh at his enthusiastic but clumsy turns, I felt a little better. I resolved that I would absolutely *not* make an unauthorized visit to Anna and Grace's safe house tomorrow morning.

"Hello, Grace. I'm Ms. Hollings. I'm Ms. Jackson's friend."

"I know who you are." The answer surprised

me. Not the content so much as how readily she gave it. Rose had described Grace as reluctant to talk, and I hadn't even tried pressing her yet. As a compromise with my guilt over the dangers of using my abilities on a child for the first time, I'd decided to try to get her to talk on her own first.

"You do?" I asked.

"You're the Angel of Mercy. Did you get my letters?"

*What?* "I don't understand."

"I couldn't send them to you, but I thought 'cause you're an angel you could read them anyway."

I felt totally thrown. Since about three that morning, when I'd awakened with the certain knowledge that, resolution or not, I was absolutely going back to Anna and Grace's Balboa Island apartment this morning, I had practiced this session in my head. What I would say and what I would ask. Then, practically the first thing out of Grace's mouth had been so unexpected, I didn't know how to proceed.

Anna, currently relaxing in the bedroom, had been surprisingly sanguine about my appearance, even before I pressed her. She told me she had slept well the night before for the first time in months, and that she really did feel better for having finally gotten her story out. That had gone a long way toward making me feel better about my decision to ignore Rose's orders and come back on my own. But now…

"I'm not an angel, Grace. I'm a regular person, like you and Mommy," I said cautiously. "Did you write letters to an angel?"

Silence greeted my question, and I could see speculation in the huge eyes. Was this stranger trying to trick her? Considering her likely history with strangers, Grace's trust was probably not given easily or often.

Finally she spoke. "Is it a secret? God won't let you tell about being an angel, will he?"

"I'm not an angel," I repeated stupidly. *Now what do I do?*

To my relief, she nodded. "Okay." I didn't know if she'd accepted my statement or had simply decided to keep my "secret." It didn't really matter, as long as I could get her to trust me.

"Grace, will you sit down and talk with me for a little while?" I indicated the sofa, and she wordlessly climbed up and settled herself on one end. I sat down on the other end and faced her. I didn't want to jump right into the topic that would be the most likely to upset her.

"You know that Rose—I mean, Ms. Jackson—

is helping keep you and your mommy safe, don't you?"

"She lets me call her Rose," said Grace in her piping voice. "But I have to remember to use 'Mrs. Jackson' in front of the other kids."

I grinned inwardly. So much for Rose's position on female authority figures. "Well, if Rose says it's okay to use her first name, you can use mine, too. Would you like to call me Mercy?"

She gave it some thought before answering, then nodded. "Okay, Mercy."

"And you know Rose is your friend, and you can trust her?"

She nodded solemnly.

"Well, I'm your friend, too. And I want to help keep you and Mommy safe, just like Rose does."

"My friend?" Her brow furrowed. I wondered who else had told her they wanted to be her friend, and if this was the wrong approach. I hadn't planned to press her so soon, but I decided on the lightest possible touch.

"Yes, Grace, I'm your friend. It's okay for you to talk to me, and to tell me things. Do you understand?"

"Yes." It was instant, and I feared I had pressed too hard. I didn't think I could do it any more subtly than I had, so I dropped the press entirely and went on.

"I want you to tell me about your daddy."

Again the tiny brow furrowed. "My daddy?"

"Yes, Grace. Please tell me about your daddy. About the things you do together."

"I'm not supposed to talk about it."

"Yes, I know. But you know how I just said it's okay for you to tell me about things?"

"Ye-es," she said hesitantly.

"Well, that includes things about you and your daddy." I didn't want to press again and hoped the previous instruction would suffice. "Okay?"

"Okay." She took a deep breath, and I could see that even with the confidence of the press behind her, she was steeling herself.

"Daddy says I'm his special girl. He loves me more than anyone in the whole world." I decided that Rose hadn't been precisely accurate when she described Grace's eyes as belonging to someone very old. I would have said changeable. Sometimes they did seem to convey the knowledge of the ages, but at others they were as open and innocent as a doll's. And sometimes, like now, they were opaque and guarded, like shuttered windows.

"He likes to take me places. We go in the car."

"What kinds of places?" I asked.

"Sometimes we go to restaurants. I can have anything I want to eat. And sometimes we play vacation."

"Vacation?" I wondered what this meant.

"Yes, like when you pretend you're in a different place. You bring a suitcase and stay."

"Stay where?"

"In a room. In a ho—ho—" She stopped, and I realized she didn't know the word.

"A hotel?" I supplied.

"Yes."

The throat lump from yesterday was back, and I swallowed with difficulty.

"Grace, when you and Daddy go to the hotel, do you each have your own bed? One for you and one for Daddy?"

"No. Because we're on our honeybun, and when you're on a honeybun, you have to be in the bed together."

*Honeybun?* "Do you mean honeymoon?" My chest was starting to constrict, and I wondered if this was what it felt like to have asthma.

"Daddy says it's okay if I call it a honeybun."

*I'll just bet he does.* "When you and your Daddy are…are pretending to be on your…your honeybun…" I wasn't sure I could get the rest of the question out, especially with Grace looking at me expectantly. I tried to take a deep breath, but the air seared my lungs as if I were in the middle of an inferno instead of a cool, quiet apartment with air that held the faint tang of salt water.

"When you and your daddy pretend to be on your honeybun, what does your daddy do?"

For the first time in our conversation, Grace squirmed and dropped her eyes. "I'm not supposed to tell."

"Grace." I said her name softly, and her gaze returned reluctantly toward my face. Releasing what I hoped was only the merest whisper of the press, I said, "It's okay to tell me. You will feel better when…when you tell me all about it."

The shuttered eyes blinked, and for a moment I got a glimpse of what Rose had described. Knowledge that no six-year-old should ever have acquired peeked out from behind the barrier, and the pressure in my chest threatened to burst my heart.

"Daddy…" she said slowly, "is the husband and I'm the wife. We have to take off all our clothes, and then I have to tickle Daddy in his special place. Then he…he tickles me in *my* special place." As I watched, horrified, both her eyes filled with tears. "But it doesn't tickle. It hurts." One tear spilled down her cheek.

I resisted the urge to grab her and pull her toward me, shushing her before she could say any more. I needed to know it all. "Did you tell your daddy he was hurting you?"

"Yes. He said mommies have to do it anyway, and that they get used to it and then it doesn't hurt anymore. But I didn't get used to it." Her voice got very low, and I had to lean forward to hear. "Not yet."

# 9

Dear Angel of Mercy,
Are you in disguize? Its okay if you cant tel me.
I unnerstand.
Love, Grace

Anger has always been my enemy. For over
half my life, it was almost impossible for me to
speak in anger without pressing. And after my
adoptive parents had returned me to the State of
New Jersey, I'd been an angry kid.

I had caused people to lose their power of
speech, jump off precipices and try to perform
anatomically impossible sex acts before I gained
a little control over this particular aspect of my
ability. It was amazing that I'd gone twenty-nine
years before anyone actually died as a result of my
rage.

Now the cold fury that welled up through my

body and made me shake like a jackhammer set red lights flashing in my mind. Since the object of my wrath wasn't available, I might take it out on the closest target. Like Anna, for not standing up to Phil. *I have to get out of here. I have to be far away from Anna and Grace before I lose control.*

"Grace," I breathed, "Grace, we are going to take a break now. I want you to…to relax and play for a little while. If Rose calls or comes by, don't tell her I was here, okay? Let's keep it a secret for now."

"Okay. I'm good at secrets."

"Yeah, me too." I felt a little steadier now, but I still had to get out. "I'm going to talk to your mommy for a minute, all right?"

"All right."

I got to my feet and stumbled to the bedroom door. Opening it, I called, "Anna?"

"Yes? Are you done?" Anna, who had been lying on the bed reading, put down her book and sat up, swinging her legs down to the floor.

I nodded. "Yes, for now. I may…I will probably come back later this afternoon. In the meantime, if you talk to Rose or to anyone else from Haven House, you won't tell them I was here." I tried to keep my press light, but with the anger running through me like wildfire, it was almost impossible, and I saw her wince.

"I won't tell."

"Okay." I dug in my pocket and pulled out a business card. "Here, this has my cell-phone number. Put it someplace where no one else will see it. Does Rose come by every day?"

Anna shook her head. "No. But she usually calls."

"I want you to call me after you talk to her. To let me know whether she will be stopping by." Again I saw a physical reaction to my press and knew I was slamming against her mind like a slap. I had to leave. Now.

I almost ran for the door, but I managed to stop and say goodbye to Grace before I fled down the stairs to the quiet alley. I practically sprinted the six blocks to the ferry, and then I stood at the rail in the front and let the salt spray sting my face during the short trip across to the peninsula. No one spoke to me, even the ferry operator who took my fare. I was sure my posture was telegraphing "stay away" in six-foot flashing neon.

Sam's gas dock and boat rental business almost directly adjoined the ferry ramp, and I was afraid he would hail me as I stepped off. I hurried past to the closest side street, staying on the opposite side of the road from Jimbo's, the pizza shop and the coffee house, any of which might contain friends or acquaintances at any given time. *Just let me get home without seeing anyone I know.* By some miracle, I made it.

Cupcake didn't greet me at the door—Sukey had a key and must have picked the mutt up to keep her company on the drive to Riverside—and Fred was nowhere in evidence. I walked rapidly around the living and dining areas, closing all the blinds tight. Grace's voice echoed in my mind. *I didn't get used to it. Not yet. Not yet. Not yet.*

I sank onto the sofa just in time for a sob to break through the pressure in my chest. It tore from my lungs painfully, sounding like a low scream.

Inarticulate sounds were wrenched from my throat as I sobbed uncontrollably. I picked up a sofa cushion and squeezed it to my chest. I rocked and screamed and howled. Tears seemed to actually spurt from my eyes. My nose ran, and I let it.

The cries hurt my throat, and I hiccupped and choked, but I couldn't stop. Finally, somehow, I pulled myself into a ball on the sofa and, impossibly, fell asleep.

I awakened to a sandpaper tongue licking my face. I would have liked to think Fred was trying to comfort me, but it probably had more to do with the salty tears that had dried on my cheeks.

"Hey, furball." I squeezed him, and he squeaked in protest. "How long has Mama been asleep? What time is it?" I searched for my cell phone, feeling the rise of panic. Could I have slept through Anna's call?

I found it still in the pocket of the jacket I was wearing. The history showed no calls that day, and a wave of relief washed over me. It was only two-thirty, so Rose probably hadn't been in touch with Anna yet. I went to the bathroom and washed my face. I didn't look as scary as I feared. My eyes were a little red, but I hadn't been wearing any makeup that morning, so there were no black streaks. My hair was flattened from my nap, but I pulled it into a loose ponytail and went to the re-frigerator to scrounge up some lunch.

*Shit.* In the hubbub of the last few days, I had forgotten to go to the grocery store. I had picked up some emergency coffee at the tiny local grocery on the next block, but I preferred to do my regular shopping at the less expensive chains on the mainland.

I didn't want to get in the car and head too far away—if Anna called, I wanted to be able to be there in a few minutes, and the ferry was by far the fastest way to get to Balboa Island on Sunday, provided one was on foot. I decided to get a sandwich at one of the bay-front restaurants near the ferry ramp.

I found a pair of sunglasses that were relatively unscratched and put them on before heading out the door. The clouds that had made that morning's air chilly had dispersed, and it was warm enough to sit on the upstairs patio of the Newport Landing to order my grilled fish sandwich.

"Hey there." I looked down at the sidewalk and saw Sam peering up at me, his hand to his brow to shield his eyes from the sun. I wondered if he'd spotted me all the way from the gas dock.

"Hey yourself." I wasn't sure whether I was happy to see him or not. I didn't feel angry anymore, at least not in that physical, visceral way I had earlier. But I might not be ready to be around other people just yet.

"Mind if I come up?"

*Hell.* If I said no, I'd have to explain why. "Sure. Want me to order something for you?"

He shook his head and disappeared from view. Within moments he came through the patio doors and sat down opposite me. "I stopped by your place earlier, but Fred was the only one home."

"I was visiting one of the women from the shelter," I surprised myself by saying. "I need to go back. I'm waiting for her call." I nodded at the cell phone on the table.

Sam frowned, but before he could say anything, a waiter appeared and took his order. A stray cloud temporarily blocked the sun, and I took off my dark glasses.

Sam, having finished his interaction with the waiter, returned his focus to me and seemed about to say something when the lines of his face changed to concern. "Geeze, Mercy, what's wrong with your eyes?"

*Oops.* I guess that in natural light they were redder than I thought. "Nothing, Sam. This morning's…session got a little emotional, that's all."

"And you're going back?" He reached for my hand, and I managed not to pull it away. "You'll wear yourself out."

I didn't want to have another argument with him, but I wanted him to understand that I wasn't going to back down on this. I picked up a fork with my free hand and played with it.

"Sam." I began, "you know I mostly grew up in foster care, right?"

"Yes," he said. "You've told me that. But not much about what it was like."

"Yeah, well, I don't really like to talk about it.

It was pretty awful, but it was a lot worse for others than for me."

"Why is that?"

The waiter appeared with iced teas, and I waited for him to put down the glasses and leave before responding.

"I was a little tougher than some, I guess. No one ever hit me, at least none of the foster parents did, and the kids who picked on me didn't usually do it twice." I took a sip of my tea. He waited. Sam was a patient listener and had that knack of keeping silent so someone else would feel compelled to speak. I wondered, fleetingly, where he had learned that.

"Anyway, like I said, there were others who didn't fare as well. Most of the foster parents were okay—kind people who meant well, even if they didn't have the time and resources to give us the attention we needed. But there were some…" I broke off, remembering. Still he waited.

"I guess most state systems are shorthanded, and they don't all have the resources to check up on people as thoroughly as they'd like. So if someone is smart enough to get around the system, they can do it."

"Like who?" Sam was paying very close attention, but his tone was mild.

"Like people who want to hurt or exploit children. And the kids are so starved for attention, they make easy targets."

Sam was still holding my hand, and he squeezed it a little. "But no one ever…hurt you?"

"No. A couple tried, but I…I shut them down pretty fast." *And, with any luck, they're still trying to figure out how to fuck themselves.* "Sam, you're right that I really don't have time to volunteer right now. But I feel as if I only survived as well as I did because I was…different. Tougher. I was lucky, and these women didn't get any luck. These children don't deserve…" I hadn't really thought things out in words, and I was having a hard time explaining myself.

"I get it," said Sam. "I know why you're doing this."

I was surprised. "You do?"

"Yeah. You're doing it because you can." He released my hand, and I searched his face for any sign of irony. I found none.

A strong gust of wind hit the patio, sending a few napkins to the floor. I shivered. It had been warm when I sat down, but the sun was starting to move lower in the sky, and I was drinking iced tea. The waiter popped his head out the patio doors and said, "Your sandwiches will be up in a few minutes."

"Are there empty tables inside?" I asked him. "Or we could eat them at the bar. It's getting kind of chilly out here." I looked at Sam. "Do you mind?"

"No, I'm kind of cool in just a T-shirt. Let's go in."

We arrived at the bar simultaneously with our plates, and I took a bite of the excellent fish.

"Look who's here." Sam gestured across the rectangular bar to where Hilda and Tino were sitting in the other room. Tino's face was turned up toward the television, where what looked like a martial-arts movie was playing, but Hilda had spotted us and was waving us over.

My plan for a solitary lunch already shot, I bowed to the inevitable and carried my plate to their table in the lounge, where a few members of the reggae band were just arriving to set up for the evening show, which started and ended early on Sundays.

"Sam, have you seen this movie? Man, this dude is powerful. Watch this next scene. He's going to kill that ugly motherfucker with a single strike to the throat." Tino mimed a karate move, and Sam obligingly watched the fight scene. When the promised kill-strike came, he laughed aloud.

"Tino, that's a bogus move. That wouldn't kill the guy, it would just piss him off. You have to crush the windpipe if you really want to stop someone. You don't hit from this angle." He imitated the actor's move, stopping millimeters from Tino's throat. "You have to come in this way." He rotated the angle of his arm so that the slice was coming in from both a different direction and a different elevation. "And you have to follow through, as if you were aiming for something about four inches behind the throat. Otherwise you'll just wound him." Sam tapped the spot where the death blow would presumably have snapped Tino's neck, had this been a real fight, and Tino's hand reached up to feel the vertebrae.

"Really? Where'd you learn how to do that, man?"

*Yeah, Sam, where'd you learn how to do that? The same place you learned Arabic?*

Before I could pursue this intriguing line of thought further, my cell phone trilled. I looked at the display, then realized I wouldn't recognize Anna's number anyway. "Excuse me, guys, I need to take this." I punched the button to engage the call and stepped swiftly back to the patio. "Hello, this is Mercy."

"Ms. Hollings? It's Anna."

"Hi, Anna. What's happening? Did Rose call? Is she coming by?"

"She called, but she's busy at the shelter and can't come by today."

It was what I had hoped to hear. "I'll be there in a little while then, Anna. Don't go anywhere." I couldn't press over the phone, but…

"I never go anywhere," she replied, and I felt a pang of sadness. No, I didn't suppose she did.

I ended the call and went back to finish my lunch, although the moist fish now felt like sawdust in my mouth. Sam was watching me carefully.

"Was that the call you were expecting?"

"Yeah," I said, putting down the sandwich in defeat. "I need to go."

I dug in my pocket for some cash, but Sam placed a hand on my wrist. "No, let me get this. You take care of business, okay?"

I felt a rush of warmth for him. How could I have been angry with a man this perfect?

"Okay. Thanks, Sam."

"Call me later. Let me know how it went."

"I'll do that." *Maybe.*

I hadn't had a lot of time to think about what I was going to ask Anna and Grace on this second session, but I made a mental checklist as I shivered on the ferry.

I didn't want to completely ignore Rose's wisdom. The graphic details of the abuse should be uncovered by experts in treating sexually abused children. Not only was I no expert, I was afraid I wouldn't be able to hold in my rage if I had to listen to the whole awful story.

But I did plan to unearth a few more facts before I confessed to Rose. *If* I confessed to Rose. I hadn't yet gotten around to figuring out how I was going to handle that detail. Meanwhile, Anna had said that Grace had told her she went out with Daddy to "visit friends." I needed to find out what that meant—who these friends were and what had happened on the visits. And, most especially, I wanted to know exactly how to find Phillip Green.

By the time I reached the door at the top of the stairs, I had convinced myself I could get the information quickly and get out. Then, once I was back home, I could decide exactly what to do with it.

My knock was answered immediately, and I was surprised when the door opened a crack to reveal an eye that peered out at waist-level.

"Mommy, it's my friend Mercy." Grace swung the door wide to reveal Anna at the kitchen counter. She almost smiled at me. Almost.

"Do you want me to go back in the bedroom?" Anna asked.

I nodded and pressed lightly. "Just for a few minutes. But I want to talk to you, too, as soon as I'm done talking with Grace."

She put down the dish towel she had been carrying and complied, closing the door behind her.

"Grace, come sit with me on the sofa. I need to ask you just a couple more questions, okay?"

"Okay." She sat on the sofa and looked at me solemnly. Her eyes were as unguarded as I had yet to see them.

"When you and your daddy go out in the car, do you ever go to visit other people?"

The shutters closed a crack. "Uh-huh."

"What happens on those visits?"

She squirmed. "We play TV."

I was surprised. "You watch TV?"

"No, we *play* TV. Like when you pretend you're on a TV show."

This was odd. "Tell me about playing TV. Who plays with you?"

"There's lots of people. But they're not all in the TV show. Some of them do the cameras and turn on the lights."

Realization dawned. "You mean like making a movie?"

She nodded. "But it's on the TV." I understood. Someone was using a video camera and viewing the playback on a television monitor. Fuck. Phil was letting someone make videos of his six-year-old daughter.

"Is your daddy in…in the TV show?" I wanted to gag.

"Sometimes." She had gotten very quiet.

"Who else is in the show?"

"Daddy's friends." Her gaze dropped to a sofa cushion.

"Do Daddy's friends…play honeybun in the show?" I swallowed and tasted bile.

She shrugged. "Sort of. It's not the same."

I stopped. It wasn't just that I didn't want to hear the details, it was that I was treading into an area that should probably be handled by a child psychologist. But I did want to identify the players, if at all possible.

"Did you go to a hotel to play TV? Or was it a house?"

She hesitated. "I don't know. It was a big building. I don't think no one lived there."

*Maybe some kind of commercial building.* "A warehouse?"

"I don't know. What's a…a where-house?"

"A big building where people store things."

"Store?" I realized I was just confusing her. She obviously didn't know enough about buildings to answer the question. I tried another approach.

"Grace, the other people that are…that are in the TV shows, do you know their names?"

"Not the grown-ups."

My heart gave an irregular beat. "What did you say?"

"I don't know the grown-ups' names. But one of the other kids is Jason."

*The other kids. Oh, God.*

After a long moment I said, "Thank you, Grace. I think that's enough questions for today." I got up on shaky legs. "Anna," I called. "Can you come out now?"

The bedroom door opened, and Anna appeared. Grace got up and headed into the bedroom, seemingly intent on a stack of books I could just see on the bed.

"Anna," I said, taking a pen and small pad from my jacket pocket, "can you tell me your home address?" I recognized the name of the street she recited; it was a middle-class neighborhood in Costa Mesa.

"And what about where Phil works?"

She shook her head. "He's self-employed."

"He works at home?" Her earlier statements had led me to believe he wasn't at the house a lot.

"No, he goes out and meets people. I don't know where."

"Just exactly what kind of business is he in?"

"I don't know."

I was about to ask how she could be married to a man for over six years and not know what he did for a living, then reconsidered. "You must have had some idea—a guess, even."

She hesitated. "I think maybe it was something illegal. He said things about some of the men he worked with, like people should be afraid of them."

"Did he mention any names?"

"I don't think so."

I put away my pad. "Thanks, Anna. I'm going to go now." I applied a light press. "Remember, please don't mention my visits today to Rose."

"I won't."

As I reached for the doorknob, she spoke again. "He'll find us, you know. And take us back. Or kill me and take Grace."

It was on my lips to tell her she was wrong, but what if she wasn't? Rose had implied that Phil had connections, and he *had* found Haven House.

"Anna, if Phil finds you, you don't have to go

with him, and you don't have to let him take Grace. You don't have to let that…that bad man have power over you or your daughter. He deserves to be punished, and you deserve to be safe." There was heat in my words, and I realized I had given an unintentional press. No harm done, probably, but my anger was rising again, and I needed to leave.

As I headed down the alley in the direction of the ferry, I thought about Grace's last statement. *The other kids.*

It had to be stopped. I didn't know where, or how, or who the other players were. I didn't know whether I had enough to take to the police or, if not, how to get it. But I knew one thing.

Phillip Green would be stopped. One way or another. *You won't hurt her again, you son of a bitch. Her or any other child.*

# 10

Dear Angel of Mercy,
Mommy is beter today and says she is not so scared no more. I am still scared sometimes but not as much becuase I know you are watching over me now for sure. Mommy and me are going to make pop corn and watch the Wissard of Oz on TV and have hot chocklat.
Love, Grace

"I'm just lucky the woman is totally anal. She kept copies of all her records and didn't get rid of them when she retired. She's got them all labeled and alphabetized, sealed in plastic tubs and arranged on shelves in her garage." Sukey shook her head, and her red curls, which she had styled so they looked like loose springs, bobbed and danced.

I hadn't told her about yesterday yet. She had

bounced into the office in such a good mood, justifiably proud of the results of her first "interrogation." I was trying to focus on what she was telling me, but lack of sleep, combined with the greasy feel of loathing that had clung to me since I left Anna and Grace the evening before, made me a poor listener.

"I had to take everything to a Kinko's and make copies, and bring them all right back. I was terrified I would get something out of order, and it's a good thing I was careful, because she inspected every file folder when I got back, one by one."

She plunked a pile of papers down in front of me, and I jumped, spilling coffee.

"Geeze, Mercy," she said, yanking back her precious papers to avoid the mess, "you're really on edge this morning. What's going on?"

I got up and retrieved paper towels from under the alcove sink. "My mind is elsewhere, I'm afraid. I need to get it together, though, because my clients are going to start arriving soon."

"Anything I can help with?"

I thought about it, and my eyes fell on the bright yellow cover of *The Exciting World of Private Investigation,* which held pride of place next to the computer keyboard.

"Yes, actually there is. I'm wondering if you

can use your newfound skills to help me track someone down."

"Sure. You can find anything on the Internet. What's the name?"

"Phillip Green. And I have an address for him. But he hasn't been staying there for a week or two, so what I'm really trying to find is if he owns any other property, maybe a warehouse or something."

After starting to call Rose and hanging up without leaving a message—twice—I had found myself in the car at about eleven the night before, driving toward the suburban address Anna had provided. I'm not sure what I thought I was going to do when I got there, but I had told myself it wouldn't hurt to just drive past and get a look at the place.

It was an unremarkable house in a very average neighborhood, the only notable difference between it and its neighbors being an absence of landscaping. The other houses on the cul-de-sac had shrubs and ornamental palms, banners and decorative mailboxes. A few children's toys were in evidence, and the house next door had a basketball hoop and backstop mounted above the garage door.

Phil's house—I couldn't think of it as belonging to Anna and Grace—had only a featureless lawn and empty driveway stretching from its neatly painted exterior. All the window shutters were closed, and no interior lights burned.

He could have been asleep, his car hidden in the garage, but I spotted a pile of newspapers spilling from the front step. I looked for a place to pull over, but there was no street parking, and even though the place looked deserted, I didn't want to park in the driveway. I had been suppressing fantasies about having a little chat with Phil all evening, and that meant I definitely wasn't ready to meet him. Yet.

I remembered what Rose had said about Tiffany's husband. *A lot of people in your position would try to handle matters on their own, and likely as not make things worse. It's natural to want to defend the victim and go after the abuser, but it's usually not the best way in the long run.*

But how could things get any worse for Anna and Grace? Other than having Phil find them, and—after a conversation with me—he wouldn't be going anywhere near them. Or anyone else.

A response to my ethical dilemma was postponed by his probable absence.

"Mercy!"

At Sukey's voice, I snapped back to attention. "Sorry."

"You said you had an address?"

"Yeah." I got the pad out of my jacket pocket. "I'm interested in anything you can tell me about him. Can you work on it today?"

She frowned. "I was planning to start running down the foster parents on these lists. Some of them may still have the same phone numbers."

"This is more important."

Her eyebrows lifted in surprise. "More important than tracking down your past? But you said…"

"I'll explain as soon as I have a break between clients, but you're going to have to trust me on this, Sukey. It's urgent."

"Okay," she said reluctantly. "I don't suppose you have a middle initial? It's a pretty common name."

"No, sorry." I should have asked Anna. I supposed I could call her later, but what if Rose was there?

My client arrived and our conversation was cut short, but as I closed the therapy-room door, I could see Sukey already tapping away at the keyboard. I doubted she'd be able to find anything useful, but it was a start.

When my client was done and we emerged together into the waiting area, Carl from downstairs was on his knees next to Sukey's chair, pointing at something on the screen.

"Oh," said Sukey, "are you done with your session already? I thought it had only been a few minutes. This is so interesting!" She stopped to collect a payment, and Carl got to his feet.

He discreetly waited until the client had left and closed the outer door before explaining. "Sukey asked for some help with a public-records search. Which I'd never done before, but it's really cool what you can find out about a person."

"Are you getting anywhere?" I asked, not really expecting anything.

"I think so. I know Phil's middle initial now— it's H—and a bunch more stuff. We can go over it at lunch. Carl's been *amazing.*"

Carl's blush rose to his bald head, and I turned toward the coffee machine so he couldn't see my smile. Sukey had obviously made a conquest.


"Mercy, that's the most horrible thing I've ever heard." I had told her what I'd learned from Anna and Grace, and as a result the lion's share of Sukey's lunch sat untouched on the table between us. "You have to call the police."

"Yes, I plan to. As soon as I talk to Rose. She's not going to be happy about me hypnotizing Grace."

"Whatever. You can handle her being pissed. And if Anna doesn't want to bring charges, you can make her. She *has* to bring charges."

I took a sip of my tea. "It'll be tricky. The only proof of the incest is going to be what Grace has to say, and having said it to me is not going to be enough. I don't even know how that works—Child Services has to get involved, I'm sure. And if the police don't pick Phil up immediately, or if they can't keep him in custody, Anna and Grace may be in danger."

Sukey sighed. "It's got to be possible to work it all out. But where do you start?"

"With Rose, obviously. Even if she wants to strangle me, she'll know what to do next."

"You left a message?"

I shook my head. "No. I should have, but I didn't know what to say. I guess I'll keep trying until she answers the phone. It hasn't even been twenty-four hours yet."

"Well, in the meantime, let me show you what Carl and I found out about Phil."

The nose-ringed waitress interrupted, indicating the hardly-touched food. "Was everything okay? You didn't eat much." We ate here often enough for her to know we usually left shiny plates.

"The food was great as usual—we're just not very hungry," said Sukey. "Can you wrap this all up? I'm sure we'll be famished later."

The emptied table gave Sukey room to spread out various printouts, and I learned Phillip H. Green had been arrested eight years ago for receiving stolen goods. "Did he have to go to jail?" I asked, shuffling the other pages, looking for something about a trial or a sentence.

"No, he arranged some kind of plea bargain and just had probation and community service. But look at this." She moved a page to the top.

The form was headed City of Newport Beach, and it took me a moment to realize what I was looking at. Once I did, I looked up at Sukey with the first genuine smile I'd had in days. "Phil owns a building that's zoned commercial? Where is this? I don't recognize the address."

"I looked at a map before we came over here— it's off Pacific Coast Highway, a couple of blocks back, kind of near the Arches."

"Geeze, Sukey, that's only about a mile from here. I wonder what kind of business it is."

"I don't know—I didn't find any permits or anything. He could be renting it out to someone else, in which case he's just the landlord, so there wouldn't be anything else in his name."

"Well, there's one way to find out. I could drive over there after work and check it out. Maybe hang around and see if I can spot him." I stopped, realizing I didn't know what he looked like. *Damn, another thing I should have asked Anna.*

Sukey sat up straight in her chair and beamed. "Do you mean you're going on a *stakeout?* Mercy, please, you *have* to let me come with you!"

"Whoa, it might turn out to be a retail store or some other business where he never even goes. Or it could be empty."

"But you *might* have to do a stakeout. Come on, Mercy, I wanna go. Please?" Sukey gave me the pleading look that had probably been getting her what she wanted since infancy, and I laughed.

"Okay, okay, you can come. But don't be too disappointed if it turns out to be nothing."

The building on which Phillip Green had been paying city taxes for the past two calendar years was the last at the end of a row that housed a hammock manufacturer, a machine shop and a defunct marine-supply store. At eight o'clock, no cars were left in the parking lot, except for what looked like a delivery van next to the hammock place. And a dark blue late-model sedan outside the building we were watching. The three of us—

Cupcake was sleeping in the backseat, snoring quietly.

"Do you have a flashlight?" Sukey asked from the passenger seat.

"Sure. There's a little one in the glove compartment," I said. "But I'm not sure you should get out of the car."

"I'm not. I want to check something in the book, and I don't want to turn on the interior light." I didn't have to ask which book; Sukey had scooped up *The Exciting World of Private Investigation* before locking the office on our way out.

We were parked in the shadows of a palm tree behind a locksmith shop, the back of which faced the alley perpendicular to the street where the building sat. We had been there for about an hour and, other than Sukey writing down the sedan's license plate number, had done nothing. She had wanted to go feel the sedan's hood, to see if it was still warm, but I had vetoed the idea. It was parked right next to the building's back door, and I was afraid someone would come out while she had her hand on the car.

She held the penlight under her chin as she looked through the pages of a chapter, then checked the index. "Shit, I can't find anything about it here."

"Can't find anything about what?"

"About what to do if you're on a stakeout and you have to pee."

At the words "have to pee," Cupcake stopped snoring and lifted his head. "Woof?" he said, clearly interested.

"I'm guessing a man wrote that book," I said. "Probably pisses in a cup or out the car door."

"Yeah, well, I can't do either," said Sukey, "but I can hold out a little longer. So can Cupcake, right, pup?" She reached back and rubbed the top of his head, and he put his chin back down on his huge paws.

"That gives me an idea," I said. "Have you got Cupcake's leash?"

"Sure. Why?"

"I'm going to take a look around. And if someone comes out and catches me, I can say I'm just taking the dog for a walk." I peered up at the lights from the houses that were perched above us on a cliff, in the section of town called Newport Heights. "We're close enough to those houses that it's not that far-fetched."

"Why do you get to go?" Even in the dark, I could hear the pout in Sukey's tone.

"Because if I get in trouble I can press my way out of it, and you can't."

"Wait!" she said as I reached for the door handle. She reached up and slid the switch on the interior light to the off position. "Okay, now you can open the door."

Although it was unlikely anyone was watching—there were no windows on this side of the building—it was probably standard stakeout procedure. "Good thinking," I said, as I closed the door as quietly as possible, then let Cupcake out of the back and snapped on his leash.

"Come on, mutt, and no barking." I walked along the street and stepped into the alley. I kept walking past the sedan, feeling self-conscious despite my apparent lack of an audience, then turned quickly down the space between the two buildings. There were two windows on this side of the warehouse, and faint light spilled out from between the slats of ratty Venetian blinds.

"Cupcake, sit," I whispered. Once he obeyed, I released the leash and eased up to the side of the building. The blinds were closed, but there were some small gaps where the slats were broken or bent. I peered in but only saw a dark room, with light spilling from an open door at the opposite end and part of an empty hallway beyond.

The second window yielded no better results, and I returned to Cupcake, picking up the leash again. "Good boy. Come on, let's see what's around the other side."

The front windows had been covered from the inside with some kind of black cloth, obscuring even the faint light I had seen from the side. I knew there were no windows facing the side street, so I reversed directions and headed back to where I had started. Maybe I could see something through the car windows.

I approached carefully, Cupcake at the end of the leash, and tried to see into the sedan's dark interior.

*Mercy, someone's coming. Get out of sight. Hurry!* Sukey's voice sounded loud and clear in my head.

I pulled Cupcake back around the side of the building and crouched under the window I had first peered through. He whined, and I quieted him, but any noise he made was drowned out by the sound of a vehicle pulling up at the rear of the building. The engine was shut off, followed by the sound of a car door opening and slamming, then a loud knock as someone pounded on the back door.

I heard footsteps coming from the other side of the window, and stood up and peeked through the holes in the blind just in time to see the silhouette of a figure walking down the hall toward the back of the building. I heard the outside door creak open and the sound of male voices in the alley.

There was a thunk, then sliding noises. I looked at Cupcake—with his black coat, he was virtually invisible in the shadows—and hissed, "Sit." I heard, rather than saw, his hindquarters land on the ground. I inched along the building's edge and, ignoring the fluttering in my stomach, peeked around the corner.

The sound I had heard must have been the van's rear door banging open, because two men were unloading cardboard cartons. I tried to read the labels on the sides of the boxes, but the light was too dim.

"Is this all of them?" asked the taller of the two men.

"Yeah. What time should I be back?"

"Vince is bringing the new camera by sometime before ten-thirty. Mrs. D is supposed to be here with the kids around eleven. We'll start shooting as soon as we get them prepped."

"Okay, I'll be back at eleven." The shorter man walked back to the van, got in and started the engine, while his companion stood in the building's open door and watched.

Before pulling away, the van driver rolled down

the window and spoke loudly enough to be heard over the motor. "Hey, Phil, I forgot to tell you. We gotta get some money over to Joey—he's gonna run out of blank tapes before he can do this new job."

*Phil?* This was Phillip Green. Suddenly I had to pee very urgently.

"Okay, I'll drop some by before the shoot. See you at eleven." The door slammed shut, and the van drove away. I grabbed Cupcake and, fairly shaking with excitement, rushed him back to the car as fast as I could go while still being quiet.

I managed to remember not to slam the doors when letting Cupcake back into the car and climbing into the driver's seat. I started the engine immediately, as Sukey peppered me with questions.

"What happened? Did you see anything? Was Phil there?"

"Yes, and I heard plenty. They're going to start shooting a kiddie porn movie sometime between eleven and midnight, and we have to make sure the police are there to catch them in the act." I struggled to keep within the speed limit. "Sukey, we could put Phil in jail *and* shut down the entire operation in one shot, if we do this right."

"Where are we going now?"

"Jimbo's. We both need a restroom and a few minutes to plan this out so the timing's just right. It'll be empty on a Monday night, and it's closer than either of our places. And," I said as I turned the corner onto the peninsula, "I really need to try one more time to get hold of Rose. She needs to know what's going on."

I had a feeling that no matter how mad Rose was at me, she would forgive me if there was a chance of putting Phil behind bars. Shows what I know.

# 11

Dear Angel of Mercy,
Mommy made a cake and said we may go to a
new house soom. I hope there are other childern
at the new house and mabye some pets! You can
come see us their.
Love, Grace


"What you did was completely irresponsible.
You may have caused that child irreparable
damage. I trusted you, and you went behind my
back."

She finally paused to take a breath, and I spoke
quickly. "Look, Rose, I know you're angry, and I
have no defense. But right now I need you to listen
to me." For about the fifth time during the conversation, I wished I could use the press over the phone.

"Talk."

I hurried to obey—she'd been tearing me a new

one for fifteen minutes, and I needed to take advantage of what might be only a temporary willingness to listen.

"If we wait until all the players are in the building and call the police, they can catch Phil in the act. He's going to be there—I heard him say so myself. If they have him cold on the child pornography stuff, Anna and Grace won't even have to bring charges or testify in court."

"And how do you plan to explain why you just happened to be hanging around the building?" she countered. "It's going to come back to Anna, at least. One look at her, and the police are going to put two and two together, and the next thing you know, she'll be subpoenaed."

"I can make an anonymous call."

She snorted. "Yeah, and they're going to believe you."

"Come on, Rose, the Newport Beach police have an average response time of something like six minutes. They'll check it out whether they believe me or not."

"You need detectives, not black and whites."

I sensed some capitulation and pressed my advantage. "So I'll call a detective." I was willing to bet Sukey had Bob Gerson's cell-phone number.

She was quiet for a moment, and I could tell

she was working it out. "Even if it all comes out the way you say, they're still going to find out Phil has a wife and daughter. Eventually Anna and Grace are going to have to talk to the D.A."

"But you can control that, Rose. No judge is going to give bail to a child pornographer with a felony arrest record, not in this town. With Phil behind bars, Anna and Grace will be out of danger, and you can make sure any interviews with the D.A. are done the right way. You can get professional help for Grace."

"If you haven't already messed her up beyond repair."

I sighed. "I don't believe that, but it's beside the point right now. Phil is going to be at that building tonight, with a bunch of other perverts. And kids, Rose. They're bringing in more children. For that reason alone, they have to be stopped."

This time the silence stretched for long seconds, and I held my breath. I didn't need Rose's permission to call the police, but I wanted it anyway.

"Okay, call them. But make sure you get the timing just right. If they don't believe you and go running in there too early, they might not get enough to hold that son of a bitch. And until he's in jail, there is no way I'm going to pressure Anna into coming forward."

"I'm going to go back over there—not so close this time—and watch through binoculars. I'll call as soon as the children arrive. The police should get there before they start filming, but if everything's already set up, it should be enough to prove what's going on."

"Maybe I should come with you."

*Shit, that's all I need.* "No, I already have someone coming along." There was no chance of getting Sukey to stay behind without pressing her.

"Well, call me and tell me how it goes. No way I'll be able to sleep until I know what happened."

"I will."

"And, Mercy?"

"Yes, Rose?"

"This thing about going behind my back and hypnotizing Grace—we're not done talking about that yet."

She hung up before I could respond. I closed the phone and put it back in my jacket pocket. I got up from the booth where I'd been sitting, as far from the front door and the bar as possible. Jimbo, who had been a saloon owner long enough to know when someone needed privacy, had made no move toward me while I was on the phone, but now he pointed to the beer tap.

"Want one?"

"Not tonight, Jimbo. Got any coffee?"

"Sure." He poured me a cup of the foul-smelling brew, and Sukey popped in the side door, followed by Butchie.

Butchie had retired a few months earlier, when he had sold his gas dock and boat-rental business to Sam. Sukey had gone to borrow binoculars from him.

"She won't tell me why you need them field glasses," he said to me without preamble. "So I came to see what's so secret that Sukey won't talk about it."

"Nosy old coot," said Sukey, albeit with affection. "Jimbo, can I have a Coke?"

"Soda for Sukey and coffee for the Newport Bitch. Borrowing binoculars on a Monday night. This have something to do with that book you've been lugging around, kid?" Jimbo waggled his eyebrows at Sukey as he placed the Coke on a coaster ostentatiously, waving off her attempt to pay him.

She grinned like the Cheshire Cat. "Maybe."

"If you girls are planning something *clandestine*—" Butchie pronounced the word with mock drama "—you should call Sam. Never hurts to bring in an expert."

"Sam?"

"Sure. He did some kind of covert stuff back around the first Gulf war." He must have noted my astonishment. "Oh, he wasn't supposed to talk about it—top secret, I expect. But his dad knew something was going on and told me about it a couple years back. He was real proud of Sam."

Sam's father and Butchie had served in Korea together. Russell Falls now suffered from Alzheimer's and probably talked when he shouldn't.

"I don't want to bother Sam with this," I said slowly, trying to absorb the import of what had just been said. Something covert? *Something that involves speaking Arabic, no doubt.* "It's his dad's caregiver's night off, and he'll be staying over there tonight."

"Besides, Mercy and I have it handled. And we'll take Cupcake for protection." The rottweiler was currently sitting outside Jimbo's back door.

Butchie made a derisive sound. "Cupcake? What's he gonna do, lick someone to death? He's about as fierce as a kitten."

"Hey, Cupcake's got skills you don't know about," said a familiar voice, and I turned to see Tino approaching the bar, followed by Grant. "Set 'em up, Jimbo. I'm buying."

"The girls here ain't drinking tonight, but I'll have a snort with you." Jimbo took down the bottle of Jack Daniels. "We celebrating something?"

"Nah, not really," Tino said. It looked as if a flush was stealing up from under his T-shirt, but it may have been a reflection from the red neon Budweiser sign.

"Tino just took his equivalency test," said Grant, quietly enough so that Jimbo, who'd poured Tino's drink and gone to fetch the good scotch from the other end of the bar for himself and Grant, couldn't hear. "And he's pretty sure he aced it."

"Man, I *killed* it," said Tino. "There's no way I failed. I probably got the all-time record high score." He glanced over at the empty pool table. "Hey, *Mamacita,* you wanna play some pool?"

I glanced at the clock. I was itching to get back to Phil's place, but it was still too early. The closer to showtime we arrived, the less chance we had of someone noticing the parked car. But I was way too edgy to feel like shooting pool.

"Sukey will play with you, Tino." In response to her questioning glance, I said, "There's plenty of time."

Tino pushed coins into the slot, and I heard the balls tumble as Sukey went over to rack them. Grant sat down on the stool she had vacated.

"Why're you here with Tino, Grant?" I asked, more to cover my nervousness than anything else.

"I drove him. He was too keyed up, plus he wanted to go over some last-minute stuff in the car."

"Oh, I forgot to mention, I saw a help-wanted sign at the car wash. If he's serious about getting out of the gang…"

Grant laughed. "Tino working in a car wash? I don't think so."

"I guess I don't see it, either. But he's not qualified for anything else."

"Are you kidding? Tino's been a gang leader for almost six years."

"That's hardly something you put on a résumé, Grant."

He took a sip of his drink, and I heard Sukey crow over a good shot. "Think about it, Mercy. For the past five years, Tino has been managing a volatile group of associates, getting them to work as a team instead of killing each other. He's had to run a business and out-think the competition, and in the meantime, he had to keep an eye on the members of his own organization who would like to replace him at the top. I've talked to him about it—he's expanded his territory and tripled the size of his business. It's a pretty impressive record."

"You're talking about running a Chicano street gang, Grant, not General Motors."

He shrugged. "A lot of successful CEOs use the same skills. But you're right, you can't walk into a company with a GED and a felony record and get hired. That's one of the reasons it's so hard for a guy like Tino to go legit. No job he's offered is going to present a challenge. He'd be bored out of his mind and end up right back on the street."

"So what's the solution?" I enjoyed talking to Grant—he had his own perspective on things.

"For most guys, who knows? For Tino, it's going to have to be some kind of business he can start up and run himself. Like buying old apartment buildings, getting them fixed up, renting them out. Something like that."

"Doesn't that take a lot of money to get started?"

"Less than you think. Tino's got some stashed, although he can't spend much without raising red flags with the IRS. But he can always get investors."

"Like Hilda?" I wasn't at all comfortable with the idea, although Hilda could probably buy ten apartment buildings for the amount she spent annually on clothing and jewelry.

Grant shook his head. "No, I told Tino it's not a good idea to shit where you sleep."

I almost choked on my coffee, and Grant clapped me on the back. "Sorry, Grant. That just struck me as funny. I wasn't sure you knew about—"

"About Tino and Hilda?" He shrugged again. "Sure I know. She's not making a secret of it."

"I always thought—" I thought better of what I had been about to say, but Grant picked right up on it.

"That I'm interested in Hilda?" he finished for me. "I'll tell you a little secret, Mercy." I looked up, and his eyes actually seemed to twinkle. "You know what one of the skills was that made *me* a successful businessman?"

I shook my head, and he continued.

"Patience, Mercy. Patience."

"What if Phil doesn't come back?" Sukey voiced what I had been fearing.

Several vehicles were parked outside the building, including the van I had seen earlier, but the dark sedan I had to assume was Phil's car was not in evidence.

"He'll be back. He was taking some money to someone, but I heard him tell the van driver he'd see him later." I felt a brief pang that I hadn't returned in time to follow Phil—whoever was making copies of the tapes should be arrested, as well—but I put the thought out of my mind. What was going to happen here tonight was the important thing. Phil would return. He had to.

I looked at the time display on my cell phone. Eleven-twenty. I had already set up my phone so that Detective Gerson's caller ID would not show who was calling, and I had written down the number of the detective bureau at the Newport Beach Police Department, just in case he didn't answer his phone. But unless "Mrs. D" had come early, no children had yet arrived. And there was no sign of Phil's car.

"Here, let me take a turn with those." Sukey gestured toward the heavy binoculars, and I willingly passed them over. She peered through them, resting them on the partially opened window for stability. Almost immediately, a pair of headlights turned the corner nearest the building and slowed down.

"I see it," she said before I could comment. "It's an SUV—a Lexus, I think." The big vehicle, which I thought might be silver, pulled up near the other cars.

"Someone's getting out of the driver's side... oh, the passenger door is open, too. The driver's a man, and the other one's a woman. They could be Asian—what do you think?"

She passed me the field glasses, and I focused on the woman's face. "Yeah, I think so. Wait, she's opening the back. *Oh, shit.*"

"What is it? What's wrong?"

I swallowed bile and handed the binoculars back to her. "The children have arrived. You watch—I'm calling Detective Gerson."

I almost punched the Send button—I had entered the number into the phone a half-hour earlier—but Sukey put a hand on my arm without removing her eyes from the binoculars. "Wait. Phil's still not back."

My finger hesitated over the phone. "Yes, but if we don't call—"

"I know." A big tear slid out from under the rubber guard on the binoculars' eyepiece. "That little boy looks about six or seven. And the girl isn't much older—nine, maybe. God, Mercy, how can people do stuff like that to innocent children?"

"I don't know." I tried to remember the exact words of Phil's conversation with the van driver. Something about shooting starting after they were done "prepping" the kids. I wondered what the hell that meant.

I made a decision and put the phone down on the seat. "Sukey, I'm going in." I reached for the door handle. "I'll send you a telepathic message if I'm in trouble or if they're starting to—to do something to the kids. You can just punch the button. Or you send me a message if Phil shows up and hit the button then. But in the meantime, I'm going to make sure they aren't hurting the children."

"Are you crazy?" She put down the field glasses and stared at me like I'd grown a third eye. "Those are criminals in there. They probably have guns and things. And if they're the kind of people who would hurt children, just imagine what they'll do to a grown woman."

"Sukey, if I get into trouble, I'll use the press. I'll be fine. I just don't want to call the police until Phil is here—they need to catch him for me to be sure Anna and Grace are safe. But I can't let anything happen to those kids in the meantime. I just can't."

Her mouth snapped shut, and I saw more tears in her eyes. "You're right," she almost whispered. "You can't."

I gave her arm a squeeze, then slipped out of the car and into the night.

# 12

Dear Angel of Mercy,
I am thinking about the new house all of the time
now. I will put your pitcture in my room and a
pitcure of Mommy and me. I can have a swing and
a slide for the other childern and for me to all play.
Love, Grace.

"Mercy Hollings, you have lost your fucking
mind," I muttered under my breath as I crossed the
parking lot adjacent to the one where we had set
up our stakeout. Once I got past the ratty row of
eucalyptus trees, barely registering the ubiquitous
scent of their leaves, there wasn't a lot to shield
me from view. I was grateful to be three blocks
back from Pacific Coast Highway, because the
streetlights were sparse here.

The only door I'd seen used so far was in the
back of the building, so we'd set up our line of

sight based on that. The door in the front, next to the taped-over windows, didn't look like it was ever opened and there was little to no chance it was unlocked, but I needed to give it a try anyway. I took the alley to the street that fronted the building and, with a prickling at the back of my neck as if an army of unseen pedophiles were watching me, slid up to the door and put my hand on the handle.

It was a glass door, with dark cloth taped over it like the adjacent windows, and still had a faded store-hours decal on the glass from a previous incarnation. I reflected that it was a crappy location for a retail store and wasn't surprised when the door didn't open.

I slipped down the side of the building opposite the cross street and again peered into the windows at which I had listened earlier. I got the same view of an open doorway and an empty hall, but this time a lot more light spilled into the corridor.

*They've set up the lights for filming.* I meant to just think it, but I must have sent the message to Sukey, because I heard her voice in my head.

*I hope that doesn't mean they're getting ready to start.*

*They probably won't start until Phil gets here,* I replied, but I didn't have much confidence in this statement. Taking a deep breath, I stepped out from around the edge of the building and into the parking area. *I'm going to see if the back door is unlocked.*

*I don't remember seeing the last group knock. Or unlock it with a key.* At Sukey's message, I tried to remember, but I wasn't sure, either.

*It might have happened when we were passing the binoculars back and forth,* I told her. There was no point stalling. I stepped onto the small cement slab in front of the door and put my hand on the knob. Ignoring the swirling ice water that had suddenly filled my stomach, I applied gentle pressure.

It turned.

I was so startled that I almost lost my grip, and it snapped back to its original position with an audible click. It took everything I had not to bolt back to the shadows, and I could feel the blood pounding in my temples.

Nothing happened. I took another deep breath.

*Sukey, it's unlocked. I think the lights are coming from the front of the building, so hopefully everyone's up there. I'm going in.*

I waited for her to argue with me. She didn't.

*Be careful, Mercy. And let me know the second you want me to make the call.*

I nodded to myself, wondering if she was watching me through the binoculars. Of course she was. Before I could lose my nerve, I grasped the doorknob tighter and turned it. As soon as I felt the click of the latch coming free, I pushed the door open and peered inside.

The door opened onto the corridor I had glimpsed through the blinds. It was empty, but light was spilling from a door at the opposite end and to the left. On my right, I could see an empty doorway into a room that had to contain the window I had looked through. Suddenly overcome with terror that someone would appear through the door at the opposite end of the hall, I pulled the outer door closed behind me and darted through the doorway to the right. I stood in the darkened room, trying not to pant.

*You okay?*

I jumped. Although I knew Sukey's voice was coming through my mind, it had sounded like she was standing next to me.

*Yeah, I found a place to hide.* I looked at the hinges where the door had been removed and glanced around the room for something substantial behind which to crouch if necessary. I didn't see anything. *For now. Don't talk to me for a couple of minutes. I'm going to try to hear what they're saying.* I wasn't sure how a telepathic message could drown out actual sound, but it was hard for me to hear Sukey and listen to anything else.

I eased as close to the doorframe as possible. The murmur of voices was audible, but I couldn't make out words. I also didn't hear any children's voices. I didn't know if that was a good sign or a bad one.

I wasn't going to be able to learn anything if I didn't leave my refuge. I leaned out into the hallway far enough to examine the other three doors leading off the corridor.

The doorway through which the light streamed was the only other open one. The one almost opposite my current vantage wouldn't get me any closer to the sound. Maybe I could just stay in the hallway.

Peeking back toward the closed back door, I stepped as soundlessly as possibly into the dimly lit passageway. I crossed to the opposite wall and pressed my back against it, then inched crab-like toward the bright illumination that was now to my left.

The voices became more distinct. A man said, "Up and to the left," and the quality of the light changed slightly.

*I think they're still setting up,* I told Sukey. *We may have a little more time.* I had drawn even with the other closed door. I gauged the angle and decided there was probably no way I could open it without being seen from the room where they were preparing for shooting.

The man's voice was suddenly very close. "That's good, Joe. Just load the tape and we can get started." I heard footsteps and realized the speaker was about to step into the hall. The bitter taste of panic rising in my throat, I launched myself across the hall and opened the door, stepping in and closing it behind me in one swift motion.

I froze. I was face-to-face with the Asian woman I had seen through the binoculars. Behind her, the two children sat on cushions, playing quietly with something on the floor between them.

"Who the hell are you?" Her voice was heavily accented.

I hesitated. I realized the flaw in my plan—I had said I would use the press but hadn't thought about what I would say.

"Listen to me," I started, and her face took on an expectant look. Before I could think of how to continue, something struck the back of my head.

A starburst of pain exploded around me and I caught a glimpse of the floor coming up fast. Then everything went black.

Something was buzzing in my ear, and I reached up to swipe it away. Except I couldn't move my hand—either hand. Through the fog that seemed to wrap around my head like cotton, I realized my arms were tied to something. An attempt to lean forward showed me it was the chair I was sitting in.

I blinked, and a face came into focus. I was expecting the Asian woman, but instead it was the man who had been driving the van. Was I gagged? No, I could lick my lips.

*Mercy! What the hell is going on?* Sukey's thought almost snapped my head back with its intensity.

*I got hit on the head,* I thought.

I was buffeted by another message. *Mercy? Can you hear me?*

*Yeah, I said I was hit on the head.* I wondered if my annoyance was telegraphed as clearly as her panic.

*I can barely hear you. Did you say you were hit on the head?*

*Yeah.* My grogginess must have been affecting

the strength of my telepathy. I tried to push a little harder, and a wave of pain in my skull almost made me vomit. *I'm tied up, but just give me a minute to press this guy and I'll be okay.* I had another thought. *How long was I…off the air?*

*Maybe five minutes. I called Bob.*

I was alarmed. *Did Phil get here?*

*No. But I just couldn't wait any longer.*

It was exhausting to keep trying to communicate this way with fresh waves of pain accompanying every thought.

*Okay, Sukey,* I managed. *Gotta concentrate on this guy now.*

The guy in question had apparently noticed my growing alertness, because he was watching me intently, his eyes slightly narrowed.

I tried to speak but only a croak came out. I saw amusement in his expression and felt anger welling up. I wet my lips, swallowed and started again.

"Untie me." I pressed, not even trying to modulate the flow.

He looked at me impassively. Was I so weakened from the blow to the head that I was incapable of pressing? "I said untie me!" I pressed so hard it should have made him flinch. He didn't.

*Not again.* Only once before had I met someone I couldn't press. And I'd ended up having to kill him.

*"Mai kao jai."* I blinked. I didn't even know what language he was speaking. A suspicion began to dawn.

"Do you speak English?" I asked him, watching his face for comprehension. I saw none.

*"Mai kao jai,"* he repeated.

*Oh, great.* If he couldn't understand me, then I couldn't press him. Or could I? If I could get him to understand my intent, did the actual words really matter?

I looked intently at his face, lifted my eyebrows, then deliberately looked down toward where my legs were bound to the chair. I couldn't really see them—there was something tied around my chest and the back of the chair that prevented me from leaning forward—but I hoped he got the message as I returned my gaze to his face. "Untie me," I said, trying to put every ounce of my intent into my tone and expression. "You want to help me get out of this chair."

His face changed slightly. Complacency was replaced by—what? Puzzlement, perhaps. He glanced down at my bound legs. Was I getting through?

"That's right. You want to untie my legs." His

gaze shot back to my face, and he searched it as if trying to pull meaning from my words by force of will.

*"Kae ja bok arai mai sarp?"* he said, and I could hear the interrogatory tone.

"Yes," I said. "You know what I want. I want to be untied, and you want to help me." He got to his feet, and my pulse, easily discernible by the pounding in my head, increased its tempo. "Come on over here and untie me. That's it."

He took a tentative step, and Sukey's voice filled my head like a flood. *He's back! The sedan just pulled up, and he's getting out of the car.*

*Good. Then he'll be here when the police arrive.*

I heard the back door open, and a voice said, "I'm back. Did you start without me?" Footsteps echoed down the hall, pulling my guard's attention away from me and toward the door. He opened it and looked out.

"Where the hell you been?" said the shrill accented voice I recognized as belonging to the Asian woman. "Why you no answer your phone? This woman show up, we don't know who she is."

"She a cop?" was his first question.

"No, we take her wallet. No cop stuff."

"Untie me!" I shouted in the direction of the

open door. I didn't know if I could press someone who couldn't even see me, but it was worth a shot.

I was rocked by another thunderous message from Sukey.

*The cops are almost here! A bunch of cars are turning the corner from PCH. I'm getting out of the car.*

"No, Sukey, stay back! Let the cops handle it!" *Shit.* In my agitation, I had shouted aloud instead of sending the message telepathically. I heard a scuffling in the hall, followed by the bang of a door, then the sound of an engine starting. There was the sound of tires spinning on gravel; then the engine sound faded.

"Where you think you going!" screeched the woman, still out of sight. At that moment, I heard a loud pounding coming from the other direction.

"Police! Open up!" It was muffled but clear.

My guard, taking one glance over his shoulder at me, leapt from the room and turned toward the back door. He shouted something incomprehensible, presumably to the woman, and I heard them running, first in the hallway, then on gravel.

*They're getting away,* I sent to Sukey. *Aren't the police coming around the back?*

*Yeah, but they're not there yet. I see them! Two people, running down the alley!*

*"Stop!"* It was Sukey's voice, and I was hearing it with my ears, not my mind. "Cupcake, piston! *Piston!*"

"You really need to have that head looked at," said Detective Bob Gerson.

"I'll go to the E.R. after we're done."

We were sitting in the detectives' room at the Newport Beach Police headquarters, less than five miles from the crime scene. It was three in the morning, and I was exhausted. Bob should be, too, but he'd just made what had to be an enormous bust by Newport Beach standards. He looked completely alert.

I hadn't used the press at all during my questioning, although I'd been sorely tempted. For one thing, our conversation had been recorded, and I didn't want to be heard giving instructions on the tape. For another, the truth would need to come out eventually, in order for Phil to be found and prosecuted. So I'd omitted only the telepathic communication between Sukey and me from my account of what had happened that night.

Oh, and the fact that I'd shouted the word "cops" and given Phil the window he needed to escape before the police surrounded the building. I'd neglected to mention that little detail, as well.

"I really need to speak with Anna and Grace," Bob said for at least the twentieth time. "I could charge you with obstruction, hold you until you tell me where they are."

"But you won't," I said, not bothering to press, even though the tape recorder was off. It was true—he owed me for this arrest, and he knew it. "Besides, I wouldn't tell you anyway, at least not until Phillip Green is in custody."

He got to his feet, and I followed suit. "Need a ride to the hospital?" he offered.

I shook my head. "No, Sukey is waiting for me in the car. And Cupcake." Sukey's questioning had taken less time than mine—she hadn't been inside the building and had less to tell.

"That mutt ought to get a medal." Bob grinned, showing slightly crooked teeth. "I thought the guy would shit himself, that big dog holding him down like that, not letting go even when the woman tried to kick him. Where'd he learn to do that?"

"Long story."

"Hey, Gerson, you're on TV. You, too, Ms. Hollings."

We walked out to where we could see a TV mounted in the corner of the big room.

A banner across the screen said Breaking

News—Child Pornography Ring Foiled in Newport Beach Bust, and the familiar face of a local
reporter filled the screen.

"Luckily the police, who were responding to an
anonymous tip, arrived before the actual taping
could take place and found the children un-
harmed—this time."

My guilt at inadvertently spooking Phil was
somewhat assuaged by the knowledge that my
arrival had probably been the reason the produc-
tion was delayed.

"Here's some video from earlier this evening,
as Newport Beach Police take away six people
arrested in the late-night raid. Five men and one
woman are in custody, and two children, a boy and
a girl aged eight and ten, have been turned over
to Family Services until their identities can be
verified and their parents found."

The screen filled with a shot of a uniformed
cop putting a handcuffed man into the back of a
car, while Bob Gerson stood to the side, confer-
ring with several other uniforms. Moments later
I emerged from the building, and he broke off to
walk over to me before the two of us headed
toward another car. The camera zoomed in on my
face, and I heard the reporter's voice say "…iden-
tified as Mercy Hollings, a local woman who ap-

parently found out about the taping and went into the building to try to stop it."

"Oh *shit,*" I said aloud. I didn't like the idea of having my face all over the news.

"That ought to get you a few new clients," said Bob, echoing my thoughts on what Sukey's take would be on the television coverage.

"Yeah, maybe. But that's not particularly how I want to get them." I waved goodbye and headed for the door.

Sukey was in the parking lot, yawning but awake. Cupcake gave a couple of wags of his stumpy tail but did not otherwise stir in the backseat.

"You're on the radio," she said, starting the car. "I hope you're not mad that I gave them your name."

"They would have found out anyway," I said. "And I'm on TV, too."

"Excellent!" she said, sounding way too enthusiastic for the hour. "Everyone will see it."

"Yeah," I said, then froze as a thought hit me. "Oh God, Sukey, Anna and Grace may have seen it. They'll know that Phil got away, and they may decide to run."

"Should you call them?"

"No, if they haven't seen it yet, I don't want to wake them up." I thought for a moment. "Let's drive over there. If the lights are on, I'll go in and calm them down. If they're off, I'll call Rose, and one of us can go over first thing in the morning."

We crossed the tiny bridge that led to the opposite corner of the island from the ferry landing and drove down nearly empty streets to the alley facing the apartment. As we pulled closer, I saw Rose come down the stairs and head toward her car, parked behind the garage door.

We pulled up, and I rolled down the window. She didn't look happy to see me.

"What are you doing here?" she demanded.

"The police raided the place, but Phil got away," I started, but she interrupted.

"I know. I saw it on TV. I came over here to make sure the girl—" she gestured toward the apartment "—didn't see it and get upset."

"Did she? See it, I mean?"

"No, they were both asleep. I told Anna about it, though—I had to explain why I stopped by. She's pretty upset."

"I could go up and talk to her," I started, but her response was swift.

"No, you aren't going anywhere near her," she said. "She'll be fine."

Sukey, who had been listening silently, asked quietly, "Should we leave?"

I hesitated, but the streetlight shining on Rose's face showed an expression so resolute, I knew it was pointless to argue.

"Yeah, let's go. I've done enough talking tonight."

We had to drive around the long way, as the ferry had stopped running hours before. I decided to skip the E.R., and by the time we pulled up in front of my apartment, I was practically salivating at the thought of my bed and sleep.

But it was not to be. Sam Falls' car was parked under the stairway that led up to my landlord's more spacious quarters above, and a light shone through the window.

I guess I had a little more talking to do tonight after all.

# 13

Dear Angel of Mercy,
Are you coming to see me soon? Mommy says I have to be pashent and wait but I am geting nervus because I dont like it hear. Please come soon.
Love, Grace

I sent Sukey home with the car and the dog, and put my key in the lock. Before I could turn the knob, the door opened. Sam gathered me into his arms.

"God, Mercy, you could have been killed. Why the hell didn't you call me?" His grip was too tight to be tender, and I extricated myself and pushed past him, heading through the living room and toward the kitchen. Sam followed me.

"I didn't plan to go inside. I was just going to sit in the car with the binoculars until the police came." I pulled a bottle of water out of the refrigerator and twisted off the cap. I swallowed about half of it before coming up for air. "I take it you saw the news coverage."

"Dad had a hard time getting to sleep, and I was watching TV. He was finally snoring, so I was about to turn it off when I saw your face." He ran his hand through his hair, a gesture I had come to recognize as one of the few physical indicators of his agitation. "Shit, Mercy, they took weapons out of there. Why didn't you stay in the car?"

"Because I was afraid the police wouldn't get there in time. The kids had already arrived, and they might have been molested by the time the cops got there." He followed me back to the living room. "If you'd been there, you'd have gone in, too."

"Yeah, I would have. *If* I'd been there. Which I would have been—*if* you'd called me."

Something in his tone made me look at him— really look at him. *Wow, he's really pissed.* Not something one saw too often in Sam Falls.

"I didn't want to take you away from your father," I said. "I knew Sukey and I could handle it."

"You and *Sukey?*" He snorted derisively. "What was Sukey going to do? Beat them unconscious with her purse?"

"No, she was going to sic Cupcake on them,"

I said, feeling my own temper start to rise. We *had* handled it, after all. "Which, I might add, she did. He caught one of the bad guys. The police want to give him a medal."

"At least you had the sense to take the dog," he said, not sounding at all mollified. "Dammit, Mercy, how did you get involved with a bunch of child pornographers, anyway?" He cut me off when I started to answer. "No—don't tell me. It had to do with someone from that women's shelter where you've been volunteering, didn't it?"

"So what if it did? A little girl I've been…been counseling was *in* some of those movies, Sam. A six-year-old girl, and her own father molested her and made her a damned porno star. What was I supposed to do?"

"Call the police!"

"I *did* call the police," I stormed. "As soon as I knew for sure the whole thing was going down last night."

"And when did you find that out?"

"Yesterday afternoon," I admitted, somewhat more quietly.

"Then why did you wait to call them until last night?" he asked. "They could have set the whole thing up in advance, and you wouldn't have had to be anywhere near the place."

"Because I didn't trust them to believe me. And I didn't want them to go in until Phil—that's the kid's father—was there, so I could make sure he was arrested and the little girl was safe."

"Was he?"

"No." I felt the anger whoosh out of me like air being released from a punctured balloon. It must have been the last thing holding me up, because I sank onto the sofa, my suddenly boneless legs collapsing. "No, he got away. And it's my fault. I—I was a little disoriented, and I shouted something about the cops coming, and he took off."

Sam's eyes narrowed. "Why were you disoriented?"

"I got hit on the head. It knocked me out for a few minutes." I reached around to feel the bump at the base of my skull, wincing when my fingers found the tender flesh.

"Let me see that," said Sam, sitting beside me. Obediently, I leaned forward, knowing there was no way I would be able to convince him I was okay until he saw for himself. "It doesn't look too bad," he said, "but you should probably have it x-rayed, just in case."

"I was going to stop by the emergency room on my way home, but I was just too damned tired. And I have clients in the morning."

"It's already morning." His fingers stopped probing the back of my head, and he moved them around to take my face in his hands and turn it toward him. He searched my eyes. "I love that you wanted to run off and save those kids, Mercy. But you have to start trusting people to help you. You have to start trusting *me*."

"I *do* trust you Sam. It's just that…" I trailed off, unsure of how to finish the sentence.

"What?" he asked.

I shook my head, frustrated. "I don't know. Maybe it's because I'm used to handling everything on my own." *Or maybe it's because I don't think I deserve your trust.*

"You don't have to be on your own, Mercy. Not if you don't want to be."

And then he kissed me.

Being kissed by Sam Falls was like sinking into warm water. Like going home. With one thing and another, we hadn't really kissed for weeks. The moment his lips touched mine, I forgot how tired and frustrated I was. I opened my mouth and tasted his breath and tongue and lips, and a great surge of desire, pushed back for so many days, rose up in me like a live thing.

"Mercy," he breathed, pulling back just enough for the words to escape before capturing my mouth again and easing me back. I gave myself over to the kiss, letting go. I hadn't known how much tension I'd been holding in my body. Now I felt like a mountain river when the water below the frozen surface, infused with the first warmth of spring, pushes up and breaks the ice apart with a violence and intensity that seemed inconceivable only moments before. There were pops and cracks as the spasms and knots that had imprisoned my muscles and nerves gave way.

Another kind of warmth was welling up in me, a heat like hot coals, banked to embers, then suddenly fanned back into flame. I groaned and groped for the buttons on Sam's jeans, unwilling to wait any longer to feel the proof that his need was as strong as mine.

Feeling my fumbling hands, he pulled back to give me access. In the dim light, his eyes, usually the chambray blue of the Pacific, were the color of the darkest star sapphire.

I freed him, but before my hands could grasp him, he pulled my arms up and my T-shirt off in one fluid movement. He unfastened my bra, and, in the next moment, my breasts were in his hands.

"Ah, God, I've missed this." His voice rumbled like a wave breaking against the shore as he bent to take first one nipple, then the other, between his lips.

I arched my back involuntarily, throwing my head back. A sound came from my throat that sounded like something Fred would make, and I laughed in savage delight.

I pulled myself up so I could reach for him again. "Why," I asked, running my hands down the ridged hardness of his abdomen and under the soft cotton of his underwear, "did we wait so long, then?"

"Beats me," he managed to say as I caught his cock, hard enough to cut diamonds and hot to the touch, in one of my hands. "Let's not let it happen again." He pulled back and stood up suddenly, making me want to howl with loss. Then he scooped me up and carried me down the hall to the bedroom.

"I love it when you carry me," I said as we approached the bed. "It makes me feel petite."

This made him laugh as he slid me down, not onto the bed, but to my feet in front of him. At almost six feet, I only had to tilt my head back a little to kiss him. I put my arms around his neck and ground my hips against him. He unzipped my jeans and pushed them down to my knees, then pressed me back into a sitting position while he pulled them off, panties and all. He knelt between my spread thighs and grinned wickedly up at me.

"You first," he said, before parting the dark curls of my pubis and plunging his tongue beneath them. All the muscles in my legs clenched, and I took in a breath so big it threatened to explode my lungs. I made myself relax and accept the gift he was giving me, and I concentrated on the sensation of his mouth finding exactly the right spot. He caught my clitoris gently between his teeth, and I gasped and worked hard not to buck.

He lifted my buttocks with his hands and laved my labia, returning with each stroke to put pressure against the bud where they met. I felt moisture gather in me, and his chuckle told me he could taste my rising excitement. He redoubled his efforts, and the vortex of my first orgasm began to form, like the initial dip of the water when a whirlpool gains just enough momentum for the first tiny pull of the surface downward into its center. It dipped and teased and then, all at once, I was sucked into the full funnel of sensation, pulling a shriek from my lungs as it danced and twisted, and I threw my head back with the sheer ecstasy of the moment.

Sam's lips pulled away, and the funnel drew back into itself. I opened my mouth to protest but was stopped when his hand came down over it, still tasting of me. I clawed my way farther back on the bed, then pulled his body toward me with one hand, reaching for his erection with the other.

"Slow down, Mercy," he said, "or I'm not going to be able to last."

"I don't care," I said. "Just…just….aaahhh." I sighed in triumph as he slid, slickly and deeply, into me.

We found our rhythm almost instantly, dancing to a beat older than any song. Flesh met flesh perfectly, and I had just enough coherent thought left to wonder why I had been avoiding this. This was right. And good, just so *good*.

Sam's prediction that he wouldn't be able to last turned out to be accurate, but it didn't matter. As much as I wanted this to continue, I wanted to feel his orgasm more.

I didn't have to tell him. Every cell in my body telegraphed need in a way no words ever could. I knew the moment was arriving as surely as he did, and as he arched and shuddered, I came again in response. "Sam. *Sam!*" We collapsed in a pleasurable tangle of limbs and bedclothes.

"I'm half off the bed," said Sam, after a few minutes of languor. I was starting to doze, and his voice woke me. I pulled myself up far enough for him to rearrange the bedclothes and get us both under the covers. He took me in his arms, and I snuggled against his shoulder. I didn't remember ever doing that with any other man—not this way.

"I love you, Mercy," he said, and my brain, already moving back toward sleep, snapped awake. He'd never said that before. Had he? Was I supposed to say it back?

"Sam…" I trailed off, and he chuckled.

"It's okay, Mercy. You don't have to respond. I just had been meaning to tell you, that's all. I don't expect you to repeat it back to me like a parrot."

"If I meant it, it wouldn't be like a parrot," I said without rancor.

"Exactly." He pulled me closer. "There *is* one thing I do want from you, though."

"What's that?" I felt so good right now, I was prepared to agree to anything he asked. Almost.

"I want you to—to consider not going back to the women's shelter. Just for a while."

I waited for annoyance to flood me and was surprised when it didn't. "I don't think Rose is going to let me back, anyway. But…"

"But what?"

*But I have to make sure Grace is safe.*

Yet how could I do that? The police were looking for Phil, and I didn't have a clue where to find him, now that Sukey's one lead had been exhausted. They had a much better chance of getting him into custody than I did, and as a fugitive, he was going to have to worry about keeping out of jail and wouldn't have time to search for Anna and Grace.

Would he?

"But nothing," I said. "You're right, Sam. I loved what I was doing at the shelter, and I'll go back to it. Eventually. But right now I need to take care of my own life." *So that when I'm ready to tell you I love you, I know who I am.* What *I am.*

"You don't have to do it on your own, Mercy. There are people who care about you and want to help you. Not just me."

"I know, Sam. And I'll try to be better about letting them. Letting you. I promise."

He sighed contentedly, and I smiled and closed my eyes. I was asleep before either one of us drew another breath.

I wasn't quite sure what the dream was about, other than the terrible noise that pursued me, blasting through my head with an almost tangible pressure. I tried to bury my head, but the sound persisted.

"Mercy," said a disembodied voice. "Are you going to answer that, or do you want me to?"

I lifted my head, which was pounding. The voice was Sam's, and the terrible noise was my cell phone. I looked at the clock. 4:59. At this hour, it had to be an emergency, and I stumbled out of bed naked and searched for the source of the ringing.

I found it on the floor next to my jeans—it must have fallen out of the pocket when Sam pulled them off—and I miraculously managed to scoop it up and push the button before it stopped screeching.

"Hello?"

"Is…Mercy?" I could barely hear the voice, but I made out my name.

"This is Mercy. Who's calling?"

"You…come. Daddy is…and Mommy…hurt."

I was only getting about every fourth or fifth word, but my heart froze solid and took on the weight of lead.

"*Grace?* Grace, is that you?"

"…Mercy…Daddy…then he…a gun. Hurry!" The line went dead.

"Holy *shit!*" I started to pull on my jeans, not bothering to look for my underwear. I tossed the phone to Sam. "Sam, find the number that call came in on and call it back. And get dressed. And call 9-1-1."

To his credit, he didn't argue and was smart enough to do what I asked—in order. "The callback number is busy," he said, tossing the phone on the bed and looking around for his own clothes. He got one leg into his jeans. "What do I tell the 9-1-1 operator?"

I rummaged in the bottom drawer for a sweatshirt, found one and pulled it over my head. "I'll make the call," I said, slipping my feet into Birkenstock sandals and picking up the phone. "You drive. Shit, I need to get to Balboa Island, and the ferry's not running for another hour."

"Yeah, but we can take my boat," he reminded me. "It'll be faster than driving around."

I punched 9-1-1 as soon as we were in the car for the short ride to where his boat was docked. "I'm calling because there may be a domestic disturbance in an apartment facing the alley behind Ruby on Balboa Island. I think someone has a gun and someone might be hurt."

"We just received a call about possible shots fired at 243 1/2 Ruby Avenue. A car has already been dispatched. Are you calling regarding the same incident?"

"Yeah, that's the right address. There's a child inside—that's who called me."

"I'll radio the officers with that information. Who is calling, please?"

I hung up the phone without answering, although I was pretty sure the 9-1-1 system would already have identified my cell number. I'd be happy to give them personal information later, but Sam and I had already arrived at the marina.

We parked his car illegally behind a service door to one of the Fun Zone businesses and ran to the boat. I threw off lines while he started the well-maintained engine, and then he backed smoothly out of the slip on the glassy water. The short trip took only minutes, although it felt like a lifetime before we reached the opposite side.

"There!" I said, pointing out a private dock in front of one of the exclusive homes that had an empty slip on one side. Sam pulled in and cut the engine. Lights came on in the house as we tied up the boat and a window flew open.

"Hey, that's private property!" yelled a voice.

"Emergency police matter," I shouted back, jumping onto the dock. I turned my head and yelled to Sam, "Follow me when you're done." I took off without waiting for him to finish tying up and went as quickly as I could down the narrow boardwalk toward the nearest street access point. Cursing the Birkenstocks, I half ran toward Ruby, just as the sound of sirens became audible, coming from my right and the direction of the bridge.

# 14

Dear Angel of Mercy,
Somthing is rong. Please hurry.
Love, Grace

Balboa Island narrows at the end nearest the ferry, so it was only about a block to the apartment. Calling myself names for not taking the extra few seconds to put on a pair of running shoes, I half ran, half shuffled, toward the narrow stairs that led up next to the garage. Despite the still-dark hour, light was streaming from the windows of almost all the houses that backed up to the alley, and I saw faces peeking out between the Venetian blinds. *Shots fired at 243 1/2 Ruby Avenue.* I briefly wondered which neighbor had made the call.

Although the sirens were closer, I couldn't yet see any flashing lights when I reached the bottom of the staircase and looked up. The door stood open, but no light shone from inside. I hesitated. *Shots fired at 243 1/2 Ruby Avenue.*

"Mercy!" The voice came from my right, not from the apartment above, and I looked to see Sam round the corner at the far end of the alley, a good two blocks away. *"Dammit, Mercy, wait for me!"*

I almost did. But at that moment a cry came from the top of the stairs—a wail in that register that no one over the age of seven can reach—and I bolted up the stairs two at a time.

I was through the door in seconds and skidded to a stop almost in time to prevent my toes from coming in contact with something very big on the floor in front of me. Something heavy but slightly yielding. A body. *Dear God, no.*

"Grace?" There was no answer, and I groped for a light switch. Nothing on the wall near the door. *Shit, who designed this place?* Backing carefully away from the object on the floor, I felt along the wall on the opposite side of the door and found what I was looking for.

Light flooded the room from the overhead fixture, and it took me a moment to register what I was seeing. Kneeling on the floor on the opposite side of the body—for a body it was—was Anna. She was holding an enormous revolver in both hands, and I could see it tremble as she aimed it toward me.

"Put the gun down, Anna." I pressed without hesitation, and she placed the gun on the floor in front of her knees. She stared at me with enormous, hollow eyes.

The keening wail sounded from my left, and I turned my head to see Grace standing in the door of the bedroom. The overhead light illuminated her blond curls, making them look like a halo.

"Mommy killed Daddy," she said in a strange, terrible voice. Then her eyes rolled back into her pale forehead, and she sank to the floor.

Even though it was a lot more comfortable than the gritty environs portrayed on television police dramas, the detectives' room at the Newport Beach Police Department was getting old fast. I realized I had spent more time sitting in the chair across from Bob Gerson's desk in the last twenty-four hours than I had in my own bed.

I craned my neck to try to see where the detective had gone. I'd finished telling him everything at least an hour ago, but still he hadn't told me I could leave. I looked at the clock and groaned—it was nearly noon. I'd been here for almost six hours. My cell phone was in Sam's car or on his boat, wherever I'd tossed it.

I wondered where Sam was. The police, who

had come squealing into the alley even as Grace was sliding into a faint, had prevented him from following me up the stairs, ultimately having to put him into the back of a car to restrain him. Once they realized he was only following me and had never been inside, they hadn't kept him long. I hoped I wouldn't find him waiting in the lobby. I needed sleep and wasn't up to a conversation, not even with Sam.

At least they hadn't put me in an interrogation room. As determined as I was to be completely truthful with them, I had barely hesitated before using the press to convince them I was a witness, not a suspect, and that they could believe what I said. There was no longer any reason to keep anything from them.

Other than the fact that it was my fault Anna had killed Phil.

Sometimes it was hard for me to remember the words I had used when anger drove me to press inadvertently. Not this time.

*You don't have to let that bad man have power over you or your daughter. He deserves to be punished.*

"I didn't think you'd still be here." I looked up to see Rosalee Jackson standing not four feet away. She must have come from one of the rooms at the opposite end of the aisle that ran between the cubicles.

"Neither did I. I'm just waiting for someone to tell me I can leave." I nodded back toward the way from which she had come. "Are you here to—"

"Anna gave them my name, and they called me. I know a few people around here, so they let me in to see her. I sat in on part of her questioning. She wouldn't let me call a lawyer."

I nodded. The police had whisked me away from the crime scene and into the back of a car before I could speak with Anna or make sure Grace wasn't hurt. I had seen Anna walk out of the apartment on her own legs, accompanied by a police officer carrying Grace, and then watched them both be driven away while I sat in the backseat of an otherwise empty car, unable to press anyone to let me out to go to them.

"Is she okay?" I asked carefully. Rose was talking to me, and that was a good sign, but the set of her shoulders told me she was far from happy to be in my company.

"She just shot her husband in front of her six-year-old daughter. How the hell do you think she is?"

I felt impotent in the face of her indignation. I could press her not to be angry, then press someone on the staff to let me talk to Anna, then press *her*...

No, it had to stop. I would just have to get through this using my personal charm. The thought almost made me laugh aloud.

"Rose, you're mad at me, and I don't blame you. But no one else is going to tell me what happened at that apartment this morning. Will you please, *please* tell me what you know?"

She looked down at me, practically incandescent in her anger, but she didn't leave, and I took that to mean she was thinking about it.

"He followed you there," she finally said.

I didn't understand. "Who? What are you talking about?"

"Anna's husband. Phil followed you from the police station. He saw me come down and talk to you, and he recognized my face from the time he was at Haven House and knew he must be in the right place." There was something in her face that revealed a certain amount of satisfaction, as if she was not sorry her words would hurt me.

I was still confused. "Phillip Green was at the police station?"

"Yeah, in the parking lot. He had another car, and he was smart enough to know everyone would end up there after the porno ring got busted. He also knew you weren't a cop, so he figured you must have found out about the location from Grace. She'd been there, you see. I guess she told you."

"Yes," I replied. It was close enough to the truth, and I didn't want to stop her story.

"So he followed you. And you led him straight to them."

*Shit.*

"How do you know all this? I mean, he's dead, isn't he?"

"He told Anna. He made her sit there and listen to him, while he held a gun to Grace's head and told the whole story." Her eyes burned, and it took all my strength not to shrink away from the intensity of her gaze.

"And Grace? How is she? What's going to happen to her?"

"A little late to be asking, don't you think?"

"Just tell me." Rose winced, and I realized with alarm, I had pressed her. God, I was tired.

"She's on her way to the hospital. She's catatonic." My inadvertent press may have compelled her to continue her story, but it had done nothing to lessen her resentment. She spat the words like weapons, and they found their marks. *Hospital. Catatonic.*

"You didn't tell me how Anna is doing. Is she—just tell me how she is."

"She's in shock or something. She's terrified for Grace, which is normal, but as far as having killed Phil…" She shook her head in confusion. "She said it was easy to get his gun away, because she knew he would think she was too afraid to try. She talks about shooting him as if she's describing a trip to the grocery store. She's sorry Grace had to see it, but it doesn't sound to me like she's the least bit sorry she shot him. I was afraid the police were going to bring charges."

"Are they?" I asked, alarmed. Good God, Anna had *executed* Phil because I'd told her he deserved it.

"No, I don't think they will. The fact that he showed up with a gun and broke down the door seems to be enough for them to assume self-defense. But you never know—someone at the D.A.'s office may try to make a case."

I pushed down a sudden wave of nausea. What had I done? I'd been trying to help them, trying to make them safe. Now Anna was in danger of being charged with murder, and Grace was catatonic.

*I've got to stop kidding myself.* The well-worn grooves of my internal mantra started playing in my head, making me want to scream. *Someone always gets hurt. I've got to stop....*

"I'm sorry," I whispered, looking at Rose's face. It didn't soften. I half expected her to tell me it wasn't my fault. But it was. And, somehow, she knew it, too.

"'Sorry' don't cut it. First, you went back there without me. Second—" she ticked off reasons on her fingers "—you hypnotized a six-year-old child, something you've never done before, when I specifically asked you not to. And third, you did or said something to Anna that turned her into some kind of avenging angel. I don't know what it was, but you did something. You denying it?"

Her chin and eyebrows came up, waiting for my dissent. I couldn't hold her stare and dropped my eyes.

My defeat—for that's what it was—seemed to mollify her somewhat, because her tone lost a little of its harshness. "I can't say I'm sorry that bastard is dead. Even if we got Anna and Grace away from him, a man like that always finds someone to hurt. And it's not even that Anna was the one to kill him. But in front of Grace…"

Her voice changed so suddenly that I looked up and saw that her eyes were filled with moisture, although no tears spilled onto her mahogany cheeks. "That little girl has been through so much. *So much.* I can only pray that she's young enough not to remember seeing her daddy die. That she'll come out of this state she's in now, and that she won't have to spend the rest of her life in counseling."

"Rose, I—" She held up a hand, and I stopped. She obviously didn't want my sympathy. Angrily, she wiped her eyes and glared at me again.

"You stay away from them, you hear me? If I hear you've gone anywhere near either one of them, I'll get a court order so fast your head will spin. I'll leak it to the papers, too. See what *that* does for your *hypnotism* business." She pronounced the word like a curse.

With one final glower, she turned on her heel and marched out of the police station, head erect, her posture showing nothing of the fatigue she must be feeling. I could do nothing but stare after her.

A rustling noise made me look around, and for the first time I realized some of the cubicles were occupied and a number of detectives had overheard the entire exchange. The few faces I could see were quickly averted, and my cheeks burned. I slumped lower in my seat and waited for release.

When it finally came, I had to call a taxi to get

home. I half expected to find Sam in the parking lot but was a bit relieved when I didn't. His car wasn't next to my apartment, either, and only Fred, meowing in protest while sitting pointedly next to his empty food and water dishes, greeted my return. My message light was blinking, and I hit the Playback button.

"Hi, Mercy, it's Sukey. Don't worry, I cancelled all your appointments for today. Get some sleep, and I'll call you tonight. Love you! Bye." Her impossibly cheerful voice made me want to cry. Sukey lived in a world where a successfully rearranged schedule and a few hours of sleep cured all ills.

There were no other messages, which surprised me. Why hadn't Sam called? I picked up the phone and started to punch in his number, then changed my mind. I wasn't sure I could form complete sentences, never mind reassure someone I was okay. Especially when I wasn't. And might never be again.

I got undressed and fell into a bed that still smelled of Sam and sex and contentment. Even as I drifted into a restless sleep, I heard Rose's voice. *I can only pray that she's young enough not to remember seeing her daddy die.*

# 15

I cant rite now.

I slept through the afternoon, got up only long enough to make and consume some toast, and went back to bed and stayed there all night. The toast should have clued me in—it was what I ate when I was depressed or angry. I awakened several times from what felt like nightmares, but I couldn't remember the specifics and didn't try too hard. None of them were disturbing enough to get me out of bed.

When the alarm finally awakened me, I got up and made coffee, but couldn't seem to get in the shower. I slumped on the sofa in my bathrobe. The sun shining between the blinds meant it was probably another perfect Southern California fall day, but to go outside I would have had to put on some clothes. Instead I picked up the remote control and channel-surfed disconsolately, finally stopping on a black-and-white movie populated with actors and actresses with faces that looked vaguely familiar but to which I could not put names. I glanced at the telephone. Sukey had re-scheduled yesterday's appointments, but what about today's?

People were depending on me to help them solve their problems. But what if I screwed up? *Someone always gets hurt.* It was probably just the usual fare of smokers and dieters, people with issues I could easily handle, where nothing was likely to come up where I might do damage. But what if they weren't? What if one of today's clients had some crisis I hadn't anticipated, and I made things worse?

Even if it was just a basic, boring day, it would involve changing out of my bathrobe. Something I wasn't prepared to do right now.

The phone rang even as I stared at it, and I picked it up. "Hello, Sukey."

"How did you know it was me? I didn't send a message."

"No, but *I* must have. I was just about to call you. You probably heard me thinking about it."

"You really think so?" she asked, obviously pleased. "Well, I was calling to ask if I should drop Cupcake off on my way or bring him to the office. What were you going to call me about?"

"I'm not coming in today."

"Are you sick?" Her genuine concern made me feel guilty. "Can I get something for you?"

"No, I'm just not up to it," I said. "Some of the stuff that happened yesterday…well, it was my fault." I had filled Sukey in on the phone just a little bit yesterday morning, and the whole thing had, of course, been on the news.

"What do you mean, your fault?" She went on without waiting for me to answer. "I'll bet it wasn't. You always think that, but you're too hard on yourself."

"Not this time."

"Whatever," she said, clearly not believing me. "Anyway, I'll go in and call everyone, say there's been an emergency. Everyone will have read the papers or heard it on the news, anyway, and no one will blame you if you need a day off. I'll come over once I get everything handled at the office."

"No, Sukey, I'd rather be alone."

"So you can sit around in your robe, eat toast and feel sorry for yourself? I don't think so." She sounded almost cheery. This girl knew me way too well. "Take a hot bath. I'll bring lunch."

She hung up before I could argue further, and

I considered sending her a telepath-o-gram but couldn't summon the energy. Besides, the idea of a hot bath really didn't sound all that horrible.

By the time she arrived, Cupcake's leash in one hand and a paper bag from the corner deli in the other, I felt human. Almost.

"Okay, so tell me what's supposed to be your fault," she began. "But first, get some paper plates and napkins—we're eating on the patio. Got any beer?"

I told her the whole thing—Anna's hollow eyes as she kneeled over Phil's corpse, the gun still in her hand, Grace's collapse, Rose's accusations. My certain knowledge that I had turned Anna into Phil's executioner and, possibly, put Grace through a shock too great for her to bear.

We both ate in silence afterward, Sukey apparently thinking it all over. She washed down the last bite of her sandwich with the beer, then looked at me.

"You're right," she said, "it was your fault."

I almost choked on my beer, and she went on. "I mean, I think it's probably just as well that Phil's dead. But that woman—Anna—never would have taken away his gun and shot him if you hadn't given her the confidence to do it. Even if she did, you have to hope she wouldn't have done it in front of the kid." She shook her head. "Poor little thing. I hope she'll be okay."

She was only voicing my own beliefs, but I was still oddly disappointed. "So you see why I can't—I can't keep pressing people. I'll have to shut down the office. It's the only way."

This time she was the one who looked stunned. "Mercy, that's not what I meant at all. You're missing the whole point."

I was confused. "Which is?"

"Look, you do fine when you press people on purpose. Your clients—and those women at the shelter—you *help* them. You make it possible for them to do stuff they could never do on their own. I could give you twenty examples right now of people whose lives you changed for the better. You know it's true," she insisted, when I would have protested. "You can't close the office, Mercy. Those people need you. A lot of the time, you're their last chance."

"But what about what happened when I lost control and told Anna—"

"Did you just hear yourself? It was when you *lost control.* You don't need to stop using the press, Mercy, you have to learn to control it better."

I blew out my breath in frustration. "Don't you think I know that? I've been fighting with this thing for almost twenty years. I just think I've got a handle on it, and *wham*—something pisses me off, or I get too tired or have one too many beers, and the next thing I know, someone's dead."

"Be fair. You haven't actually killed anyone because you lost control, Mercy."

"Not technically, no. But they're still dead."

"Unless there's someone in your past you're not telling me about, Mercy, we're talking about two very, very bad guys. They deserved to die."

"Maybe. But no jury sentenced them to death, Sukey. *I* did."

"You're getting away from the point, Mercy. We were talking about controlling your ability."

"I told you—"

"I know, you've been struggling with it for twenty years. But that was on your own, Mercy. You were trying to do it without help."

"You can't help me with this, Sukey. I appreciate that you want to, but you just can't."

She shook her head. "I didn't mean *me*. I meant the others out there that are like you. The ones Dominic told you about. Your parents, or your relatives, or whoever."

I was silent. She was right. I had thought about finding these people for what they could tell me. But it had never occurred to me to think about what they could *teach* me.

"I…I don't know. I mean, we may not ever find them."

Sukey beamed and I must have looked puzzled because she laughed. "You said 'we,' Mercy. You may actually be getting the hang of letting someone help you." She finished her beer and put the can down. "But the real reason I'm smiling is that I may have already found out something really important. Just let me get my papers from the car."

By the time she got back, folders in hand, I had cleared the table, and she spread out the now-familiar piles of notes and photocopies.

"Here," she said, digging a thin folder from the stack. "This is from the first time Rocko was on parole." She opened it and thumbed through the pages. "He had to report every time he got a new job or left an old one. Sometimes the parole officer would call to verify. See here?" She pointed to an entry. "The parole officer called this guy up when Rocko reported he wasn't working there anymore, to make sure he didn't get fired because of stealing or something."

"Hanson Steeples…West Coast Amusements." The entry was dated almost fifteen years earlier. I looked up. "So?"

"So I called the phone number. It's still good,

and this Steeples guy answered. He owns the company."

"Did he remember Rocko?" I asked.

"Yeah, he did. But that's not why I think it's important. It's because of what he told me about why Rocko left." She looked up at me, her eyes sparkling with delight over revealing a fact she had dug up in her investigation.

"It seems Rocko had a friend—a guy a couple of years older than him—that he recommended for a job with the company. The two of them left together. Mr. Steeples didn't recall Rocko all that well, but he really remembered the friend."

"What about him?"

"He said he was real persuasive. Rocko wasn't such a good employee that a referral from him was going to automatically land the guy a job. But when he came in, he was such a smooth talker, Hanson hired him on the spot. Figured he'd be good at it."

"Good at what?" Sukey hadn't said what kind of company West Coast Amusements was.

She grinned. "Working the midway. It's a company that provides concessions for amusement parks and fairs. Rocko and his friend got hired as *carnies*."

Dominic working as a carnie? It didn't sound

right to me—he had considered himself such a so-
phisticate. "I don't know. 'Persuasive' sounds like
Dominic, all right, and he admitted his press was
nowhere near as strong as mine. Even so, you'd
think he would have talked his way into something a little less labor-intensive."

"Don't forget, he was a lot younger. You said
your ability got stronger as you got older. Maybe
his did, too. But it's not just the persuasive
comment that makes me think this has to be
Dominic."

"What, then?"

She pulled out some handwritten notes.
"Rocko and Ted—I think that's Dominic's real
name—were working at a good-size fair all the
way up in Humboldt County. Steeples had
provided almost all the concessions—games,
food, even sideshows. He had this woman who
worked for him who had a fortune-telling booth.
She was real popular and always did a lot of
business."

Sukey got up and went through the screen door
into the kitchen, speaking loudly so I could hear
her. "She got sick suddenly and ended up in the
hospital." I heard the refrigerator door open and
close; then Sukey returned with two more beers
and handed me one.

"Steeples was upset—her concession was one of his best earners—but the doctors told her she had to take a couple of months to recover, so Steeples was going to shut it down and take his losses. Then Ted came to him with an idea."

"I can't imagine Dominic's real name being Ted."

"I know, it doesn't fit." She opened her can and took a sip. "Anyway, Ted said he wanted to take over the fortune-telling concession temporarily. Said he knew all about Tarot cards and palm reading and stuff. Claimed to be part Gypsy. So Steeples decided to give him a chance."

I was skeptical, then thought about Dominic's dark good looks. "It sounds like a stretch. I mean, some young guy just claims to know how to do this stuff? From what I understand, Tarot's pretty complicated."

"Yeah, but don't forget the persuasive part. And as it turned out, the guy was a huge success and ended up making Steeples a bundle."

I thought about it. It made a weird kind of sense. Dominic was a telepath and, by the time I met him, a strong one. It would be incredibly easy for him to look into someone's mind, then tell them whatever they wanted to hear. Fifteen years ago, Dominic would have been—what? Nineteen?

Twenty? Maybe just starting to come into his powers and looking for an easy way to turn them to profit.

"What happened?" I asked. "It sort of makes sense, but I can't imagine Dominic being satisfied with carnie wages—even with tips—for long. He would have wanted to move on to bigger and better things."

"Madame Zelda got better. Ted had been making more money for Steeples than she ever had, but she had a contract, so the company had to take her back."

"I can't imagine *Ted* took that too well."

Sukey shrugged. "Steeples usually had more than one event going simultaneously. He planned to build a concession just for Ted—run both of them at the same time."

"Is that what he did?"

She shook her head. "He never got the chance. A couple days after Madame Zelda returned she showed up at Steeples' office. She was working a fair near the company headquarters—they all were, because Rocko was still working the game booths, and Ted had gone back to that temporarily. It seems that more than one of her regular customers had come in looking for her young 'apprentice.' They were all missing valuables of one kind or another—jewelry or cash, mostly—and they had started to remember giving the items to Ted."

"Started to remember?"

"Yes." Sukey leaned forward, excitement showing in her body language. "They told Madame Zelda they had come in for readings and later couldn't find their watch or whatever. Then, weeks later, they would suddenly remember that during the reading, Ted told them to hand the items over, and they just obeyed. Sound familiar?"

"Holy shit. It *was* Dominic."

"Yep. The bastard was using the press to rip them off."

"But his instruction to forget the whole thing only lasted a little while." I nodded in understanding. It made sense—even my strongest presses wore off eventually.

"I haven't even told you the best part. The two best parts."

"Which are?"

"Well, Steeples didn't think Ted was a very good name for a fortune teller. So when he had the banners painted to cover up Madame Zelda's signs, he gave Ted a new name."

"Don't tell me."

She smiled like the Cheshire cat. "You got it.

Dominic the Great. I almost peed myself when Steeples told me."

I felt the hair stand up on my arms. "What's the other thing?"

She wiggled her eyebrows. "Madame Zelda—that's not her real name, either. She's retired from the carnival route, but Steeples says she still works a few of the smaller shows on her own, mostly up north. He thinks if I call around to the county fairs and maybe some of the rodeos, I should be able to find her. She goes by—" Sukey peered at her notes "—Madame Minéshti."

"Madame Minéshti." I tried out the odd-sounding name on my tongue.

"I looked it up. It's a real Gypsy name. As in actual *Rom*." She looked up at me. "Do you know anything about Gypsies?"

I shook my head. "Almost nothing. Have you made any calls yet?"

"No, I just talked to Steeples late yesterday afternoon. I wanted to talk to you before I went looking."

"Of course, even if you find her, what makes you think she knows anything that will help us?"

"Because of something she said to Steeples. She told him she knew about Dominic, because she had met his kind before. Steeples said he

asked her if she meant his kind—like thieves—
and she said, no, she meant people who could
make others do their will."

A shudder ran through me. I could barely
breathe. "You don't think she means…" I stopped,
unable to go on.

"People like you?" Sukey finished. She
shrugged. "Maybe. It's worth asking, don't you
think?"

"I guess so." I exhaled slowly.

"So, you want me to go ahead and try to find
her?"

"Yes."

"Excellent!" She stood up, looking ready to
grab the phone and start dialing right away. "I'm
going to go to the office and use the high-speed
Internet to start looking for small carnivals around
Northern California."

I was about to protest that she didn't have to run
off, but I looked past her and saw a familiar figure
coming down the boardwalk, the afternoon sun
glinting off his hair.

Sam Falls was looking right at me. And he
wasn't smiling.

# 16

Dear Angel of Mercy,
Are you reading my leters? I dont think so.

Sam and Sukey exchanged greetings as she departed, and I stood awkwardly at the patio gate, trying to ignore a low thrum of uneasiness. Something about his posture told me this wasn't a casual visit. I held the gate open, and he stepped inside. He didn't hug me.

"I was going to call you when I got home," I started, "but I decided I was too tired."

He just looked at me. I resisted the urge to fill the silence. I wasn't sure why he wasn't talking, but I could outwait him. I had a lot of practice at this game.

Finally he sat on one of the old wicker chairs. I sat opposite him and waited.

I realized he wasn't trying to make me uncomfortable—he was putting his thoughts in order. I felt a flash of annoyance. He was upset with me again; that much was obvious. But he was going to retreat behind that wall of self-control and reason.

"I can't do this anymore, Mercy." His eyes were clear and blue and empty, as if all the emotion had been washed out of them.

"Can't do what?" I knew the answer, but I didn't feel like making this easy for him.

"I can't be in a relationship with someone who picks and chooses when to trust me."

"I do trust you," I said automatically. It was true. It was *me* I didn't trust.

He shook his head. "No, you don't. Not enough to be honest with me."

"You talk like there's something new I'm hiding from you. Nothing's changed since the night before last." I heard the mulish tone in my own voice and knew I was being childish. *You can't be mad at me now for something you already knew about, no matter how legitimate it is.*

"Don't be obtuse, Mercy." He ran his hand through his hair, and I felt a mote of satisfaction at this tiny chink in his armor. "When you got that phone call, I didn't argue, I just went with it. I only asked one thing—for you to wait for me before going in."

"Grace was inside," I argued. "I couldn't wait."

"I was about forty seconds behind you, maybe less. And you knew someone had a gun in there. I heard the police say shots had been fired."

"Anna wasn't going to shoot me."

"You didn't know who had the gun. And she didn't know who was going to come in that door. She could have blown your head off."

I started to argue but had a vision of Anna, crouched on the floor, the pistol aimed at my face. At the time I hadn't thought about the dark opening of the barrel, but in my mind's eye it was enormous, impossible to escape. What would have happened if I hadn't been able to press her so quickly? Would she even have recognized me in her condition?

"How would it have been any different if I'd waited?" I asked stubbornly. "There just would have been two of us in the line of fire." I winced at my choice of phrases.

"You're not trained for stuff like that, Mercy. If you have to go through a door where people are armed, there's a right way and a wrong way." A little heat had finally crept into his tone.

"I'm not *trained* for it?" I heard the note of triumph in my voice. Mr. Caution had just tripped up. "But *you're* trained for it, aren't you, Sam? You know exactly how to 'go through a door' and a lot more. But you haven't trusted me enough to tell me about it—to be honest with me."

His lips whitened. "If there's something I haven't told you, it's because I'm not able to."

I snorted. "Oh, that's rich. If I keep a secret from you, it's a trust issue. If you keep one from me, it's fucking national security or because you took some damned oath or something."

"As a matter of fact," he said, "I did take an oath." His eyes weren't flat anymore. They blazed with blue fire. Good. Angry I could handle.

"You could have told me that. You could have said 'Mercy, I was involved in something for the military or the government or whoever the hell it was, but I'm not allowed to talk about it.' I'm the last person who would have demanded details from you, and you know it." I felt like I had the moral high ground for the first time in the conversation—maybe the first time since I'd known him—and I pushed on.

"You didn't keep your secret because of some oath, Sam. You kept it because there's something about it you don't *want* to tell. Something you think is too awful to share, too big to trust me with."

My words were designed to incite, but they had the opposite effect. What little tension had shown in his body vanished, and his eyes lost their fire. When he spoke, his voice was soft. But not his intent—that was pure steel.

"There's no point arguing about whose secrets are bigger or who has a better reason for keeping them. It's not about who wins the debate. It all just goes to prove my point."

Sam had moved forward on the chair, and now he got to his feet. I stayed seated, and he looked down at me. His eyes hadn't regained that terrible emptiness, but had once again become the chambray blue that always made me think of the sea. A lump formed in the middle of my chest. His physical beauty still caught me off guard sometimes.

"We can't keep on this way, Mercy. And you're not—" He seemed to catch himself. "*We're* not willing to do what we would have to do to make it work."

I took an experimental breath to see if the lump in my chest would strangle me. It didn't—quite.

"So," I said carefully, listening for a quaver in my voice. There was none. "This is it, then." It wasn't a question.

He let out a long, slow breath before answering. "Yeah. This is it."

He took a step closer to me and started to lift his hand. For a moment I thought he would reach for my face, and I held my breath. I didn't know what I would do if he touched me. I hadn't cried in front of another person since before puberty, but I was terribly afraid it was about to happen.

To my relief, he seemed to think better of what he was doing and dropped his hand.

"I'll see you around, Mercy." He made an expression that was almost a grin but held no mirth. Then he opened the gate and walked down the boardwalk in the direction of the marina, his posture relaxed and his gait unhurried. I watched until he turned the corner.

"See you around, Sam," I whispered. I stared at the spot where he had disappeared for a long, long time.


The sun slanted across the empty fairgrounds, beams made visible by dust kicked up by the tires of the pickup truck that rattled down the deserted dirt path between the booths and enclosures. The gaily painted signs seemed faded, and the colored bulbs looked as if a fair number of them would be revealed as burned out once the fair opened its gates and the electricity was switched on.

The truck, which might once have been white, drew toward me and I stepped aside to let it pass. It slowed to a stop, and a man jumped down and picked up a bag of trash, and tossed it into the truck bed. He stepped up on the bumper and banged on the truck body, and the driver put the truck into gear and moved on toward where the next cluster of bags stood, some thirty feet farther along the track. Neither man looked at me.

I felt hollow, cleaned out. After Sam's departure, I'd surprised myself by not falling apart. Instead, I'd spent the rest of the day cleaning my neglected apartment and even vacuumed the inside of my car, then taken Cupcake on a long walk on the beach. I'd treated us both to tacos, even bringing home a fish taco for Fred, then watched some television with the cat on my lap and the dog by my feet before turning in at a reasonable hour. I had no memory of what had been on.

Putting my doubts about continuing my hypnotherapy practice on hold, I'd gone back to the office, and my day at work had been routine. Sukey was subdued—for her—and had neither asked me about Sam's visit nor commented that I was quieter than usual.

It had gone on like that for the rest of the week. Work, walk on the beach, TV, early to bed. No distractions, no drinks at the bar, no chummy lunches with Sukey, no new leads in her investigation. She seemed to know I needed a break. When, at the end of the day on Saturday, she had handed me the piece of paper with the name and address of a county fair in Eastern Oregon, she'd been un-characteristically matter-of-fact.

"It's there through the weekend," she'd told me. "Then they're packing up. Madame Minéshti is definitely with them, but she's not part of the regular crew, and anyway, the season is pretty much over. I might not be able to find her again until spring."

I looked at the scrap of paper, the information written in Sukey's familiar, looping handwriting. I'd been to Oregon, but only to the coastal cities, and neither the town nor the county was familiar.

"I'd have to leave soon," I said. "It's got to be a fourteen-hour drive."

"More like sixteen—I made a map." She handed me another sheet of paper, and I stared blankly at the page bearing the logo of a popular Internet map site. "Or you could fly into Portland or even Bend and rent a car, but I couldn't find a flight that didn't cost an arm and a leg."

I shook my head. For some reason I couldn't explain, a sixteen-hour drive sounded pretty good.

"You'd have time to check in to a hotel for a few hours, at least. The fair is closed on Sunday mornings."

"Maybe. But I think I'd rather talk to her before they open."

Sukey's gaze searched my face. "You're going, then."

"Yeah, I guess I am."

Southern California traffic isn't as bad as it's portrayed in the movies, but the highways are never really empty, no matter the time of day. Once I'd passed the Grapevine, which was the local name for the winding section of highway just above the Tejón Pass, the already sparse Saturday evening traffic diminished to almost nothing. Living in Balboa, it was easy to forget that this other California existed. I hit Modesto a little after midnight and stopped, yawning, for a cup of horrible coffee at a truck stop.

I hadn't even really considered Sukey's suggestion that I get a hotel room. For the first time in my life, I was deliberately heading toward someone who might have some answers about my origins. If I stopped, I was afraid I might turn around.

So I had driven right through, and had arrived at the fairgrounds a little after dawn.

I'd expected to find locked gates and had figured I could press whoever I found to let me in, but it hadn't been necessary. No one had paid any attention to me, including the guys driving the trash truck.

I found Madame Minéshti's tent easily—it wasn't that big a fair—but a canvas flap had been drawn across the entrance and tied down.

"Hello?" I walked around the back and found another entrance, also tied closed. Had I thought I'd find her working out of the back of a painted wooden wagon, like in the movies? Ridiculous, but I suppose that was the picture I'd had in my mind.

I looked around, frustrated. I supposed I could go check in to a hotel and sleep for a couple of hours, then come back when the midway opened and get in line with the regular customers. But having come this far, I didn't want to pause.

Something white, glimpsed between the long metal buildings that must have housed the agricultural and livestock exhibits, caught my eye. I stiffened and saw a camper, much the worse for wear, parked in a dusty space. I walked down to the end of the row, where I could round the building, and saw a small village of trailers, campers and battered motor homes. As I approached, a pit bull, chained in front of a pickup truck with a homemade camper shell, barked frantically, only to be silenced by an unintelligible shout from inside the camper.

Looking at the slavering dog, I felt a brief pang of longing for Cupcake, who probably had forty pounds on the mutt. I wouldn't tell Fred, but I was getting attached to the dog.

I wondered how I would figure out which of the homes on wheels belonged to Madame Minéshti when a door banged open behind me, and I turned to see a skinny man—a kid, really—emerge from a scabrous Winnebago, scratching a three-day-old beard and carrying a cup of coffee.

"Help you?" He looked cautious but not hostile.

"I'm trying to find Madame Minéshti. Is one of these—" I gestured to indicate the vehicles "—hers?"

He squinted a little, as if he was sizing me up. I realized the morning sun was at my back and in his eyes. I shifted to one side, not knowing if letting him get a better look at me would help or hurt.

"You oughtta come back after the fair opens," he said. "I don't think she does readings out of her trailer."

"It's a personal matter, not a reading. We—" I wondered how to put this. "I think she might be an old friend of the family." Almost true. I could have pressed him, but I just wasn't in the mood. I'd done way too much spontaneous pressing lately.

He must have decided I didn't look too dangerous, because he gestured down a row to his right. "It's an old Airstream. Probably has a blue pickup parked next to it. I ain't sure she's an early riser, though."

"Thanks," I said.

The hollow feeling in my stomach sharpened as I approached the Airstream, surprisingly shiny and dent-free despite being an obviously vintage model.

*Don't make yourself crazy. She may not know anything.*

The curtains were drawn over the windows, including the one in the door. Taking a fortifying breath, I knocked.

There was a rustling within, and a curtain was pushed aside a few inches. A voice came from behind the door.

"What do you want?" The sound was flat, without accent, which I hadn't expected. More movie stereotypes, probably, but I'd thought she'd sound Eastern European.

"Madame Minéshti?"

"Yes," she replied, then repeated, "What do you want?"

One would think that someone who had just spent sixteen hours in a car for the express purpose of having a really important conversation with a complete stranger might have rehearsed her opening lines a bit. I hadn't, opting for the distractions of late-night talk shows and obscure country-music stations.

"I'd like to talk to you." It was the best I could come up with.

The opening in the curtain got wider, but all I could see was part of a hand. Squared-off nails, no polish.

"Do I know you?"

"No," I said. "We haven't met. But you may know something about someone I…" I trailed off. What had I been about to say? *You may know something about someone I killed?* Right.

"Come back when the fair opens." The slit in the curtain disappeared entirely, apparently signaling the end of the conversation.

"I'd rather talk now. I'm not looking for a—" what had the kid called it? I wasn't sure "—for a reading."

This actually drew a laugh, faint but discernable even through the door. "I don't talk to strangers for free. Forty-five dollars."

"Fine. I'll pay for a session. Please, Madame

Minéshti, can't you just open up and talk for a few minutes?" I really didn't want to press her. Not only was I feeling generally reluctant, but Sukey's account of her conversation with the old carney boss had implied that the woman within had met people who could press before. She might recognize what I was doing, and I was here to get information, not to reveal anything about myself.

But I *would* press her if it was the only way she would talk to me. Reluctantly summoning my power, I prepared to thrust it. I'd never tried this without being able to look into the recipient's face, but the intent ought to get through, and that's what made it work. Wasn't it?

"Madame Minéshti," I began, but stopped when, to my surprise, the door opened.

The first word that sprang to mind was dignity. This in spite of the rather shabby chenille robe and dime-store rubber thongs. It was her face.

She took a minute to study me through eyes so dark they might have been black, although I knew that was impossible. The illusion was probably caused by the canyons of bone and flesh that surrounded them, emphasized by high cheekbones and a startling widow's peak. The contrast between gray roots and impossibly black hair should have made her look foolish. It didn't. She might not sound like my simplistic idea of a Gypsy, but she certainly looked the part.

*Well, of course she does. It's her profession.*

I must have passed her scrutiny, because she stepped back into the shadows, leaving the door ajar. I had to duck to get through the doorway, but once inside, the ceiling was high enough that I didn't have to stoop. I looked around.

The place had the tidiness of a well-kept boat cabin, everything stowed away and spotless. Again, it was not what I had expected. Where were the feathers, the threadbare fringed shawls and the crystal ball? Probably in the tent out on the midway. Here, the tiny table held only a vinyl placemat printed with a cheery sunflower on which a World's Greatest Grandma mug was centered. It had been washed until the image on the side, a toddler of indeterminate sex holding a baby of equally indeterminate sex, was faded. It still held a little dark liquid, and I looked around hopefully for a coffee pot, barely managing not to sniff like a bloodhound. Nothing except a faint smell of citrus-scented cleanser. Maybe it was instant.

"Nice trailer," I said, meaning it. *I could live like this.*

She didn't respond to the compliment, but

instead slid into a seat and gestured toward the place opposite. As I complied, she moved the cup and placemat aside and reached into a deep pocket in her robe. She extracted a purple-and-gold drawstring bag, emblazoned with the symbol for a popular brand of whiskey. It didn't look new, but it was neither dirty nor frayed.

From this she removed a deck of cards, almost tenderly. Setting the bag aside carefully, she began to run the cards through her hands, closing her eyes. *It's as if she's greeting them.* As soon as the thought entered my mind, I knew it to be accurate.

Her movements changed, and she began to shuffle them as I watched, fascinated. The backs were ordinary, looking like playing cards, but the deck seemed thicker. They didn't look worn so much as somehow seasoned, like wood that picks up the patina of fingertips. Her pace increased until the cards flashed through her fingers like water.

"There is a question much in your mind," she said, and I realized I had been mistaken when I thought of her voice as flat. While she didn't precisely have an accent, there was something about the quality of the tone that brought images to mind—campfires and starry skies.

"Yes," I said, realizing she was waiting for a

response. Her eyes were still closed. "But I don't really want—"

She interrupted. "As I move the cards, you must concentrate on your question."

I stifled a sigh of impatience. I had agreed to *pay* for a reading, not *get* one. But something about the rhythm of the cards in her hands was soothing to my jangled nerves, and I felt a slight loosening of the taut wires that bound my stomach. *Why not? I really am here to ask a question, after all.*

So I looked at the flowing stream of cards as they moved through her hands and mentally conjured the words *What can you tell me about the man who called himself Dominic the Great?*

Except that's not the question that came to mind at all. My question was something else entirely.

*Am I good or evil?*

# 17

Dear Angel of Mercy,
Are you mad at me?
Grace

The thought was fully formed and filling my
mind before I even knew it. *No,* I tried to tell
myself. *That's not what I want to ask. It's...*

"Your question will be answered," said
Madame Minéshti, and she opened her eyes. I
almost opened my mouth to protest, but stopped.
Something in her gaze told me it was too late to
change the question.

She placed the cards in a perfect pile that was
centered in front of the place where my hands
rested in my lap below the table's edge. She then
set both *her* hands palm down on the table, just
behind the cards, as if guarding them.

"With your left hand, and still thinking about

the question, you will cut the cards one time." It wasn't a request.

I complied, and her gaze followed my hand as I carefully lifted a section from the top of the deck and placed it next to the original pile. The moment I withdrew my hand, she snatched the cards back up as if it had distressed her to surrender them to another's touch.

She held them in front of her heart for a few moments, her eyes riveted on mine, and I realized I was holding my breath. Then she began laying the cards on the table, face up.

They were, of course, Tarot rather than playing cards. She set them into the shape of a cross, starting with a card in the center and moving outward. The card closest to her was on its side, and the rest were upright.

"You may recognize this as a variation of the Celtic cross, although this form is far more ancient," she said, and I realized she was reciting the words without having to think about their meaning. This must be part of the routine she used for customers in the midway tent, and I suspected it was to keep them from squirming while she formulated a supposed fortune for them. "It goes back to the origins of the *Rom* in the northern part of India, when they left their homes…."

Her voice trailed off, and I saw that a vertical crease had bisected her brow. "This is very odd." The words were not directed at me, but to herself.

"What do you mean?" I asked, and her slight start surprised me. If this was part of her fortune-teller act, she was very good.

She gave me a sharp look. "Your spread." She gestured at the cards. "See for yourself."

I tried to focus on the colorful pictures. They looked familiar, or at least some of them did, but I couldn't have put a name to any of them. I'd seen Tarot cards before but had never had a reading, nor taken any particular interest.

My lack of understanding must have shown on my face, because her voice took on a mild tone of impatience. "They're all Major Arcana. There's not even a court card. And none are reversed."

"Major Arcana?" I wasn't familiar with the term.

"Non-suited cards," she explained. "Tarot cards have suits—wands, swords, cups and coins—or pentacles, as some people call them. Except for the Major Arcana, which don't belong to a suit and are generally considered to hold more significance."

I looked at the cards but gained no more understanding. "Is that unusual?"

Her eyebrows rose. "I've been reading cards for more than sixty years. I have seen this perhaps three times."

"Did I do it wrong? We can start over." If the odd configuration of the cards was going to get her too caught up in the reading to answer my questions about Dominic, it would be better to eliminate the distraction.

She shook her head vigorously. "No, these are the cards your question drew. They are the right ones. But my dear—" She looked at me searchingly, and I realized she had never asked my name.

"Mercy," I interjected, and she looked startled. I saw that she hadn't understood, so I explained. "My name is Mercy."

Her face cleared. "Ah. My dear…Mercy. This is a very powerful spread. One that holds great significance for you."

I nodded. I just wanted her to get on with it.

She pointed to the card that she had placed first. "This is your Significator. It is you, as you are today, in relation to your question."

I looked at the card. The image was disturbing. A bolt of lightning was striking the top of a tower, which was on fire. Figures seemed to be jumping or, perhaps, were being thrown from high windows, plunging toward jagged rocks at the structure's base. "It doesn't look reassuring," I ventured.

"It's not. The Tower means upheaval, and usually not a pleasant one. Maybe something violent. People hurt, literally or figuratively."

I thought about Anna, crouched over Phil's body, the round bore of the pistol aimed at my face. Hairs rose on my arms, and I shivered.

"You could say that," I said.

She eyed me shrewdly. "This doesn't have to be a negative message, child. The disturbance can be a wake-up call. The Tower may have fallen because it was really a house of cards."

I thought about my carefully constructed life. A business that might be too dangerous for the people it was supposed to help. Friends who had been in danger because of me. And Sam…

She had moved on to the card to the right of center. Two dogs—or were they wolves?—howled at a yellow moon. Water flowed around them, and something that looked like a scorpion climbed onto an island. It wasn't as threatening as the tower, but it was unsettling. "This is your past—probably your recent past as it relates to your question." She seemed to consider.

"The moon represents mystery, and your fear

of it. The moonlight is tricky—people get lost.
Maybe you got lost in the past?"

I didn't know how to respond to this, so I just
nodded. "But the moonlight is beautiful, too. You
should not be afraid of the secrets it reveals. It can
illuminate a path. In the past, you have not had the
courage to follow this path." Her finger went back
to the center card. "You've been hiding in the
Tower. But that's no longer an option."

My throat was starting to feel very dry.
Parched. I wanted water but was reluctant to ask.

"Now, your opportunity card." Her finger
moved to the card at the bottom of the spread,
which lay on its side. A frisson of apprehension
went through me as I saw what was on it. A
skeleton, clad in armor, rode a pale horse. A king
lay dead in its wake, and a figure with a hat like
the pope's offered something up before him.
Catching my eye, she went on. "Yes, Death. It sig-
nifies change. And that which is inescapable."

*What's inescapable? A death that I will
cause? My nature?*

"Not necessarily a bad thing, just something inevitable." She looked back at the previous card.
"With the other two cards, it's a potent message.
You've been living in denial, avoidance, but no
longer. Which brings us to the next card."

I looked at the card to the left of the Tower. An angel, or some kind of winged being, floated above a throng of naked people. Were they rising from coffins? Arms were outstretched in welcome, or perhaps entreaty. "What is it?" I asked.

"Judgment." I winced, and I could see she had caught my reaction, for her eyebrows rose again. "Something on your conscience, I take it. This card may mean you will be judged for your actions. Justice can never be avoided for long."

She must have noticed my distress, because her tone softened as she went on. "Or it may merely mean you have judged yourself too harshly." She looked back at the card and then to me. "I think in your case it has more to do with making a decision. Something you have been putting off, judging yourself wanting. Now it's time to commit."

*That's why I'm here.* I almost said it aloud.

"And finally, there is the card that tops the reading. Sort of a summing-up of the situation at hand. As it relates to your question, of course." She frowned. "It's very odd. Up to this point, the reading is extremely straightforward. Yet this is… more subtle."

I looked. A man seemed to be suspended

upside down, dangling by one foot. A halo shone around his head. Was he dead?

"The Hanged Man is a bundle of contradictions. He may represent a paradox."

"A paradox?" I wasn't understanding.

She made a gesture that encompassed the other cards. "These speak clearly. You must stop hiding in the Tower, which, in any case, has already collapsed around you. The mystery you fear cannot be avoided, and change is inevitable. Right or wrong, you must move forward."

She sighed and picked up the top card, peering at it as if it would disclose its mysteries. "But the Hanged Man is about pausing, letting events take their course. Taking your time. About giving up control."

I didn't like the sound of that.

"Some believe the Hanged Man is based on a real person, a nobleman who attempted to martyr himself to save his people. But he didn't die. Instead he hung suspended from a tree for days, without food or water, until he achieved spiritual clarity. Then he untied himself and came down."

"What happened," I croaked, "when he came down?"

She shrugged. "It depends on which version of the story you believe. But with this spread, I think we have to assume the lesson is that once he realized he had the answers, he came down from the tree in order to act on them."

Madame Minéshti gathered up the cards and put them back into their bag, which disappeared into her pocket, and started to get to her feet. "Now, if you will be good enough to pay me, I have things to do before the fair opens."

I reached for my wallet. "That was certainly worth the price, but it's not what I came to ask you about."

She looked surprised. "Didn't you have a question in your mind?"

"Yes," I admitted, "but not the one I intended."

"That's not unusual. You asked the question you *needed* to ask, not the one you *wanted* to."

I'd think about what *that* meant later. "Please, if I could just have a few more moments, I want to ask you about someone I believe you knew a long time ago."

"Who?" Her tone was impatient, but I could tell she was curious.

"A man who worked for the carnival a long time ago. He called himself Dominic the Magnificent."

Her face started losing color as soon as the words left my mouth. "What do you want to know about him?" she asked, her words sounding as if she had to force them out.

"Hanson Steeples said you told him something about Dominic. About his stealing from customers."

She looked at me with real suspicion for the first time. "Yes. I told him." She wasn't going to make this easy for me.

"Madame Minéshti, Mr. Steeples said you told him…you had known others like Dominic. People who could force others to do things against their will."

She stared at me, and I waited. Outside, I could hear the sounds of the campground coming to life: a door slamming, voices raised in greeting, the pit bull barking. The silence became uncomfortable, but I didn't want to speak first. Finally she sighed deeply, as if it hurt to draw air into her lungs.

"Dominic—that was not his real name, but I don't remember the real one—he was one of the others."

"The…others?" It was my turn to have difficulty breathing.

"That's what my grandmother called them. The Gypsies have names for them in the old tongue. Which I don't really speak."

"So you *are* a real Gypsy?"

She drew herself up, and some of the color returned to her face. "I am. One-hundred percent."

"And that's why you know about these… others?"

She got heavily out of the seat and went to the tiny sink. Opening an overhead cabinet, she got down two glasses, filled them with water from the tap and returned to the table. I drank mine greedily.

"Dominic was only the second I ever met. There was a woman when I was a girl…" She trailed off, lost in thought. "My grandmother said they had been around for all the Gypsies' history. They often traveled with us, pretended to be one of us. But the old ones were not fooled."

"What were—*are* they?" I asked.

She shrugged. "They looked like us. But they could do things. Not magic—Gypsies can do magic. Even if it is in the blood, magic is something you learn. There are rituals, rules. It comes from nature around us. We draw the power of the earth, of fire, of the trees. It's almost impossible to make it work on someone other than yourself, at least not without their cooperation or belief." She looked at me. "Do you understand?"

"Not really," I admitted.

"Let's take your reading. If you hadn't been ready to hear them, the cards wouldn't have spoken so clearly."

They had been pretty damned clear, I thought.

"Or curses," she went on. "You can't really put a curse on someone who doesn't believe in the magic. Then their fear makes the curse more potent."

"I see." I didn't, entirely, but I wanted her to go on.

"The power of the others came from inside them. They didn't need spells or have to draw from the elements. And when they were strong, it was impossible to resist them."

"And was Dominic strong?"

She shook her head. "Not especially. But strong enough to take advantage of those who had already come in with an open mind. But he was still a young man, a boy, really." She shuddered. "I hate to think of the man he must have become."

I thought about the adult Dominic. Amoral. Ruthless. Driven. I shivered, and she saw me.

"You know him, don't you?" Her eyes widened. "Does he know you're here?" She looked around at the door, as if Dominic might suddenly appear there.

"He's dead," I told her, and her body lost some of its tension.

"Are you sure?"

"I was there when he died."

"Then why," she asked, suspicion plain in her tone, "are you here asking me about him now?"

Suddenly I knew I was going to tell the truth.

"Because Dominic is the only person I ever met who was like me."

It took a second for my words to register, and then she almost crawled backward out of her seat to get away from me. Panic tinged her tone, and she stuttered.

"G-get *out!*" She backed toward the door and flung it open, then skittered away from the opening, pointing at it with a shaking finger. "Go *now.*" She fumbled for her pocket, as if touching her cards would give her strength.

I pressed. I hadn't intended to, but I wasn't done talking to her, and I was afraid she might hurt herself, she'd become so distressed. "Be calm," I said. "Don't be afraid of me. You can believe I mean you no harm."

Her shaking stopped instantly. She returned to the table and sat opposite me.

"You did it to me, didn't you?" she asked matter-of-factly.

I was surprised. My subjects were usually unaware that anything unusual had happened. I nodded.

"You told me to be calm. And I am. And I know you won't hurt me." She actually tittered a little. "I'd probably believe you wouldn't hurt me right up until the knife blade slid between my ribs. But I'd still believe it."

"It's true," I said, no longer pressing. "I really only want to talk to you."

"You're strong," she observed. "A lot stronger than Dominic. Or the woman I knew when I was young."

"I guess so. But I don't have anything to measure my strength against. As I said, Dominic was the only…other I ever met. And I…he died before he could tell me anything, except that I wasn't unique."

"Oh, I suspect you're unique, all right." She took a sip of her water. "The power I have—to read the cards, to perform a spell or two—it may not be all that strong. But I know power when I feel it. And yours is astonishing."

"Tell me about the woman you mentioned," I said. "What's her name?"

"She went by Helen, but I doubt that was her real name. She showed up one winter, claiming to be distantly related to a man who had been a member of the group, but had died the year before. She had all the details right—names and dates and family history."

"You were traveling?"

"No, not in the winter. There's a community outside Barstow. Some of us traveled in the warmer months, but she was gone by spring. My grandmother and some others got onto her."

"Couldn't she just have used her powers to convince you to let her stay?"

"You really don't know, do you?" She was completely relaxed now, enjoying the chat. Good.

"No. As I said, I know almost nothing."

"With the others, it's not all the same. Different ones have different abilities. Helen had attraction. Sexual attraction," she added, when I gave her an interrogative look. "She was plain to look at, but when men were around, she could put on attractiveness like she was slipping into a dress. She could seduce them in minutes, have them eating out of her hand. They'd give her anything. Afterward, they'd hang around like stray dogs."

I thought about this. I certainly had no such power. On the other hand, I had never tried. If anything, I'd sometimes made myself unattractive in order to avoid attention.

"What happened to her?" I asked.

Again she shrugged. "There probably would have been no trouble if she'd confined herself to outsiders or customers. But she made the mistake of messing with some of the women's husbands. One day, when the men were mostly away fishing, my grandmother and some of the others just grabbed her, threw her into a van and drove her to a truck stop in a town about fifty miles away. Told her to catch a ride with the next driver coming through. She must have taken their advice, because I never saw her again."

The bitter taste of disappointment filled my mouth. "So you have no idea where she might be today?"

"She'd be an old woman, if she's still alive," said Madame Minéshti. "But if she is, I'll bet she's living well, probably the beneficiary of a big fat estate or two."

I let that sink in for a while. "What about other Gypsies? Would any of them know where I might find one of the others? You said they traveled with you and passed themselves off as real Gypsies. Are some still doing that, do you think?"

She gave me a compassionate look, then surprised me by reaching across the table and taking my hand in hers. I let her. "Child, that was years ago. Even centuries. When it wasn't that easy to get from place to place, a person would need some kind of safe passage. No one paid much attention to the Gypsies, so it was probably a good way to go unnoticed. But today…"

She looked out the window, and I followed her gaze to where the highway could be seen beyond the edges of the campground. Cars and big rigs roared by. "Today it would be easy to create any identity you want, especially if you have extraordinary abilities. Gypsies don't travel so much anymore—most of them have settled in small towns, and the young people aren't much interested in the old ways. Plus you'll seldom meet a rich Gypsy." She shook her head. "No, the others have moved on. We don't see them anymore."

I gently removed my hand from her grasp. I felt hollowed out, empty as a dry corn husk. All this way for so little.

"You're disappointed."

I looked up to see her eyeing me critically. "Yes," I admitted. "I hoped—I don't know what I thought."

"You hoped I would give you the address of a whole colony of others who would take you in and answer all your questions." She stood up, picking up the now empty glasses from the table. "And I couldn't. But you did learn something you didn't know before."

I followed her example and got to my feet. "Yes."

"And don't forget the reading. The cards gave a clear message. I can't believe they would have told you to seek the mystery if you weren't going to find answers."

I turned to go, then stopped. I faced her. "Just one last question."

"Yes?"

"The others. Are they…human?"

She paused before answering. "I don't know, child. I just don't know."

# 18

Dear Angel of Mercy,
I was mad at you but not any more. I guess it is
hard to be an angel sometimes.
Love, Grace

It had been a normal week at the office, or as
normal as they get for me. Sukey had been disappointed that Madame Minéshti hadn't given me
any clues she could follow up on but was pleased
that I'd apparently decided to keep on working. I
hadn't taken any further action, telling myself I was
following the counsel of the Hanged Man. Once I
achieved clarity, I'd climb down from my tree.
Right now I was still hanging in there. Pun
intended.

"I'm meeting the gang at Newport Landing,"
said Sukey as she shouldered her purse and
clipped Cupcake's leash onto his collar. "Skip's

sister is playing her guitar at happy hour. You should come. We won't have many more warm evenings this season."

"Maybe I'll stop by in a while," I said, not really planning to. I'd been taking advantage of Indian summer my own way, mainly by taking a lot of long walks on the beach and along the bay front. Taking a step backward in preparation for two forward, or something like that. Figuring out my next move.

"Okay. See you later. Oh, I left something for you." She pointed at the stack of mail and magazines on the desk, and I nodded.

I shuffled through the stack, stopping when I came to an unmarked manila envelope. I opened it, pulling out a single sheet of paper. A Post-it note bore Sukey's familiar looping scrawl.

*You haven't wanted to talk about this stuff the last few days, but I found this yesterday. Let me know when you're ready to discuss. Love Ya!— S.*

The page was a printout from an Internet site. At the top I saw a familiar name, followed by a series of bullet points. My heart lurched.

*Mr. Thomas J. Hollings, born 1951*

It was my father. Or, rather, the man who had given up any claim to that title when he and

Bobbie had turned me over to the state of New Jersey in 1989. There was her name, too, under the bullet point entitled Spouse. My name didn't appear.

Several addresses were listed, the most current being in Arizona. There was a phone number. I went so far as to glance at the telephone positioned conveniently next to the page but quickly dismissed the idea.

If—and it was a big if—I spoke to Tom and Bobbie Hollings, it wasn't going to be over the phone.

I put the sheet of paper back into the envelope and started to leave it on the table, then folded the whole thing into quarters and slipped it into my jacket pocket. I'd think about this on my walk. I was about to turn off the light when I heard footsteps on the stairs. Figuring Sukey must have forgotten something, I opened the door.

Rosalee Jackson stood on the stair landing.

We stared at each other for what seemed like a full minute; then I stepped aside and let her in. She walked through to the therapy office, and I followed her. She seated herself on one of the comfortable chairs and looked at me expectantly. I followed suit.

"I'm surprised to see you here," I said. It was

an obvious statement, but someone needed to start the conversation.

"I'm surprised to be here." She seemed to relax with an effort, looking me over. "I was pretty mad at you, Mercy. Maybe as mad as I've ever been at anyone."

*Was.* She said *"was."* I waited.

"I thought you did irreparable damage to Grace and Anna. I still think you acted recklessly. But I've come to believe you had their best interests at heart."

"I've been pretty mad at me, too," I said softly. "And you know what they say about good intentions."

"Yeah, well, maybe this time we caught a break." She dug in her purse and took out a cigarette case. I raised my eyebrows, but she opened it up and showed me the interior. Empty. "This was a Christmas gift when I was nineteen. I can't bring myself to throw it away." She closed it and stuffed it back into her handbag.

"I was so mad, I wanted to prove to myself you were full of shit. So on the way home from the police station, I stopped at the grocery store and bought myself some cigarettes. Not just a pack, either. I got a whole carton."

She smiled wryly. "Oh, yeah, I was gonna have

myself a good old time smoking them up. Got a
fresh lighter, made a pot of coffee and turned on
*Court TV.* But you know what? I couldn't bring
myself to light one."

"You couldn't?"

"Nope. I'd put one in my mouth, give the
lighter a snap and then just sit there looking at the
flame. I just couldn't make myself inhale. Damn
near burned my thumb, the stupid lighter got so
hot. Tried for the better part of an hour before I
opened the back door and threw the whole
damned mess into the garbage can."

I felt my lips quirk. How many days since I had
smiled? "That must have been frustrating."

"Yeah." She returned to staring at me.

"You said maybe we caught a break. What
did you mean?"

She took her time answering. "With Anna and
Grace. Maybe, just maybe, they're going to come
out of this okay."

A sigh came out of me like air being released
from a punctured tire. I hadn't even realized how
tightly I'd been holding myself in.

"Can I see them?" That may have been pushing
it, but she almost smiled. Almost.

"Actually," she said, "that's why I'm here. She
asked to see you."

"Anna?"

"Grace."

I let this sink in. "Where are they?"

"Back at their house in Costa Mesa. Since Phil is dead, and it doesn't look like he left a will, everything goes to Anna. There was no reason for them not to return home."

"Bad memories, maybe."

"Maybe. For Anna, anyway. But she seems happy enough to be there, and Grace's abuse all seems to have taken place elsewhere." She got to her feet. "If you're not busy, we can go now."

"I'm not busy."

We decided to take separate cars, as she had to get back to Haven House and wouldn't be staying during my visit. I followed her to the quiet suburban street. The house looked better by daylight, and there was something else different about it.

"There's a garden!" I was so surprised I spoke aloud. When I'd visited before, the thing that had struck me was how the other houses on the street were landscaped and this one was not. But a bed of dark brown planting soil now spread away from the front door, and a row of new bushes with shiny leaves that I vaguely recognized as small lemon trees lined either side of the driveway.

Rose pulled up in front of the house, I took the empty driveway, and she met me at the front door. When it opened to her knock, I almost didn't recognize Anna.

She looked fantastic. Not that she was dressed up. Far from it, in fact. Her hair was pulled untidily into a kerchief, and her oversized sweatshirt had a big dirt smudge on the front. Suddenly I knew who had planted the fruit trees.

"Mercy! I'm so glad you came." For a minute I thought she was going to hug me. Instead, she gave me her hands, and I saw dirt under her fingernails.

It was the flush in her cheeks that made her look so different, I realized. She'd been so pale before, so colorless. "Come in," she said. "Mind the mess. I've been painting, or getting ready to."

"And gardening, it looks like." I stepped around drop cloths and paint cans into a plain white kitchen with stainless-steel appliances. Rolls of wallpaper were piled on the countertop, a few chunks of what must have been tile samples preventing them from rolling onto the floor. "You've been busy."

She blushed, and I realized she was almost pretty. "I always wanted to redecorate, but Phil would never let me. I just hate all the plain white.

The guys at Home Depot are starting to get tired of me, I've made so many trips and asked so many questions."

*Damn, she's actually chatty.* I looked at Rose, who lifted her shoulders in a barely discernable shrug.

"I'll let you two visit. I've got to get back to Haven House." She gave me a hard stare. "You call me. I want to talk to you about coming back there. Strictly on a trial basis, you understand."

"I'll call." I would, too.

"Can I get you something? Iced tea?" Anna offered.

"Water would be fine," I said. "Where's Grace?"

"In her room. Writing in her journal, I think." The front of the refrigerator dispensed ice and water, and she handed me a tall glass.

"Is she…okay?" I was afraid to hear the answer.

"See for yourself." She walked around the counter into an alcove that led into a living room. She waved dismissively at the white sofa and chairs, the chrome and glass coffee table. "I'm getting rid of all this stuff. It turns out Phil had a lot of money in the bank, and my lawyer says that since they're dropping the investigation into his death, I'll probably be able to keep it all. I may go back to school in the spring, but in the meantime, I want to make this place into a real home."

She paused and looked up at me with the first trace of a cloud I had seen in her expression. "I'm okay, really I am. I believe what you said—that I didn't deserve the way Phil treated me. But I still plan to replace everything he picked out. It's our house now. Mine and Grace's."

That said, she gave a quick knock and opened a door. "Grace, someone's here to see you."

*"Mercy!"* A tiny blond missile shot across the room and collided with my legs. Arms wrapped around my waist. "You came!"

"Hello, Grace." I felt a lump in my throat about the size of a baseball. Had a child ever embraced me before? I didn't think so. It felt…wonderful.

I disentangled myself in order to sit down on the bed. She jumped up next to me and took my hand.

"I missed you, kiddo," I said. "And I was worried about you. I heard you weren't feeling so well."

"I was in the *hop*sittle," she announced. "I don't remember very good. They said I was sleeping all the time."

"I was afraid you wouldn't wake up." I examined the tiny fingers with the little moons of pearly fingernails that looked so small in my own long hands.

"Why?" she asked.

"Well, because something kind of scary happened to you. I was afraid you were so scared, you might just keep on sleeping." Was this an appropriate thing to say? I wasn't sure, but it was the truth. I'd always wished more people had told me the truth when I was a kid.

"Oh, you mean when Mommy shot Daddy." Her countenance clouded. "That *was* scary. I was afraid he would wake back up and be mad at Mommy."

"But he didn't." I wondered if she really understood that Phil was dead.

"No. Because he died."

I guessed she understood. I looked up to see Anna still standing in the doorway, watching us. I couldn't read her expression.

"Does it…make you feel bad to remember it?" Rose probably wouldn't approve of this topic, but Grace seemed amazingly composed.

"Yes, a little." She looked up at Anna. "But Mommy said Daddy was sick. Like when you get the flu. Only his kind of sick made him want to do bad things. And he couldn't get better, even if he was sorry."

Anna and Grace shared a smile that didn't include me. I didn't mind.

"And if he didn't die, he'd keep on doing the bad things. So now he's not sick anymore."

"That's right, Grace." Anna's voice was tender.

"Mommy? Can I talk to Mercy alone for a minute?" The grown-up statement sounded funny in the child's voice, and Anna and I exchanged amused looks.

"Sure, honey." Anna stepped forward and kissed the blond head. "I'm going to wash up for dinner. How about if I order some pizza?"

"I *love* pizza," said Grace enthusiastically. Anna shut the door behind her. Grace turned to me, her expression solemn.

"Mercy?"

"What?"

"I know you're not an angel."

I stifled a laugh. "You're right, I'm not. How'd you figure that out?"

"It's in my journal." She reached over to the other side of the bed, retrieving a pink spiral-bound notebook with a teddy bear on the cover. As she turned the pages, I could see a childish but legible handwriting filling most pages. "Here it is." I thought she was going to hand me the book, but instead she read aloud.

*"Dear Angel of Mercy,"* she piped. *"If you can't come soon, please send me a friend."* She closed the book. "I think the angel sent you and made your name Mercy so I would know."

The lump in my throat was back, threatening to strangle me. "Maybe you're right," I managed to say.

"I know I am." She looked at me sagely, then grinned, and the illusion of wisdom beyond her years vanished in an instant. "Hey, Mercy, do you like pizza?"

# 19

Dear Angel of Mercy,
Thank you for helping me and Mommy and for sending my freind. Please wach over Mercy, too, becuase I think somtimes shees sad. I will hlep you wach over her and the other kids downe here. Also, Angel, plese try to help Daddy if you can. He did bad thigns but he was sick and Im afrayd he is lonly now that he cant see me no more. He dyed but maybe angels can help peepul even after they dye.
Love, Grace

"I'm so glad to hear they're all right," said Hilda. "That Rose Jackson does wonders."

"She sure does." There was no reason for Hilda to know I'd had anything to do with Anna and Grace's recovery. If, in fact, I had. I'd pressed a little self-esteem into Anna, but Grace seemed to be making her own miracles.

I'd decided to skip the pizza and join the gang at the Landing after all. Happy hour was over, but the music was playing, and everyone was still there, sitting on the upper verandah in the warmth of the outdoor heaters that just managed to abate the evening's chill. Everyone except Sam, whose boat was missing from the marina.

"So, will you be volunteering at the shelter again?" asked Grant, who was sitting between Hilda and Tino.

"Maybe in a little while. But there's something I have to do first." I pulled the quartered envelope from my pocket and unfolded it. "Grant, I know you know about this, and I think Sukey may have told the rest of you that I've decided to look for my birth parents."

"Yeah," said Tino. "You find something out about them?"

"No, not yet." I removed the page from the envelope and spread it out on the table. "But I might have a place to start."

As they all craned forward to see what was on the page—all except Sukey, who had already seen it—I went on. "I know I was abandoned. But I don't know where, not even which state, for sure. My adoptive parents—" I tapped the page "—moved around a lot. But I think they may know where I was found. I remember them talking about it, vaguely."

"Doesn't your birth certificate have a hospital or something?" asked Grant.

I shook my head. "No, just the city where the agency was located. Which is not necessarily the same place as where I was found."

"I think you're being very brave." Hilda reached out a bejeweled hand and squeezed my arm. "We'll do whatever we can to help, won't we?"

*She's really a big softie, for all her tough talk.* It was Grant's voice in my head, I realized. I looked up to see him gazing fondly at Hilda. Tino, who was squinting at the paper, didn't seem to notice.

"You gonna go see these people?" he asked. "I could come along, supply some muscle."

"Yes, I'll be talking to them. Soon—maybe next weekend. I'm going to cut back on my office hours, too, so I can devote more time to the search." I looked at Sukey. "We'll figure my new schedule out on Monday, okay?"

"Sure," said Sukey, and I realized she hadn't been paying very close attention. She was watching the top of the stairs. Expecting to see someone, I supposed. I wondered if it was Bob Gerson.

It wasn't. A familiar bald head appeared, and I recognized Carl, the graphic artist and computer guru.

"Excuse me," said Sukey, standing up and waving. "Over here!" Carl saw her and approached the table. Introductions were made all around.

"I saw your dog outside," said Carl, settling into a chair Sukey had insisted he drag over. "He's so well-behaved. Doesn't seem to mind being tied up, and a lot of people stop to give him some attention, even if he is about the size of a pony."

This comment got us to all glance over the side of the rails, to where Cupcake was tied next to the sidewalk. Sure enough, a man had stopped to scratch his head.

"You're a good boy," I heard the man say. Cupcake was tolerating the attention but just barely. He didn't seem to like the man.

Suddenly, Hilda sat up very straight. "I don't believe it," she blurted. "It's that son of a bitch Stanley Wentworth."

"Wentworth?" asked Tino. "You mean the motherfucker who beat up that chick, that Tiffany, who Mercy brought to the house?"

"The very one. I'd like to go down there and kick him right in the balls." Hilda shook a pointy shoe ominously, and I saw Carl wince.

Sukey caught my glance, and it didn't take telepathy for us to get the same idea.

"Cupcake!" we shouted simultaneously, and as the big head turned up, ears lifted, we both hollered at the top of our lungs, "Piston! *Piston!*"

# #1 *NEW YORK TIMES*
## BESTSELLING AUTHOR
# DEBBIE MACOMBER

What do you want most in the world?

Anne Marie Roche wants to find happiness again. At 38,
she's childless, a recent widow and alone. On Valentine's
Day, Anne Marie and several other widows get together to
celebrate…what? Hope, possibility, the future. They each
begin a list of twenty wishes.

Anne Marie's list includes learning to knit, doing good for
someone else and falling in love again. She begins to act on
her wishes, and when she volunteers at a school, little Ellen
enters her life. It's a relationship that becomes far more
important than she ever imagined, one in which they both
learn that wishes can come true.

# Twenty Wishes

"These involving stories…continue the Blossom Street
themes of friendship and personal growth that readers
find so moving."—*Booklist* on *Back on Blossom Street*

*Available the first week of May 2008 wherever books are sold!*

MIRA®

**New York Times** bestselling author

# MAGGIE SHAYNE

Before she joined Reaper in hunting Gregor's gang of
rogue bloodsuckers, Topaz was gunning for just one vamp:
Jack Heart. The gorgeous con man had charmed his way
into her bed, her heart and her bank account.

Now she and Jack are supposedly on the same side.
As Reaper's ragtag outfit scatters, Topaz sets out to solve
her mystery: what really happened to her mother, who
died when Topaz was a baby? And what stake does
Jack have in discovering the truth about her past?
Topaz is sure he's up to something—but her suspicions
are at war with her desires....

# LOVER'S BITE

NEW YORK TIMES
BESTSELLING AUTHOR

# Anne Stuart

Talk about lost in translation....

In the wake of a failed love affair, Jilly Lovitz takes off for
Tokyo. She's expecting to cry on her sister Summer's shoulder,
then spend a couple months blowing off steam in Japan.
Instead, she's snatched away on the back of a motorcycle,
narrowly avoiding a grisly execution attempt meant for her
sister and brother-in-law.

Her rescuer is Reno. They'd met before and the attraction was
odd but electric. Now Reno and Jilly are pawns in a deadly
tangle of assassination attempts, kidnappings and prisoner
swaps that could put their steamy partnership on ice.

# Fire and Ice

"Anne Stuart delivers exciting stuff for those of us who like
our romantic suspense dark and dangerous."
—*New York Times* bestselling author Jayne Ann Krentz

*Available the first week of May 2008
wherever paperbacks are sold!*

MIRA®

www.MIRABooks.com

MAS2536

From the author of
*Killer Focus* and
*Double Vision*

# FIONA BRAND

## SHE KNOWS HIS SECRETS....

## ONE OF THEM IS THAT
## SHE HAS TO DIE.

Within hours of finding a Nazi
World War II codebook in her father's
attic, Sara Fischer becomes a target.
Afraid for her life, Sara calls in a debt.
FBI agent Marc Bayard moves in the shadowy
world that Sara has fallen into and may be the
only one who can guide her out.

Sara and Bayard are catapulted into the cutthroat
world of international oil politics where their
survival depends on whether or not they are able
to see through the mistakes of their past.

# BLIND
# INSTINCT

"Brand's extraordinary gifts as a storyteller are very
evident."—*Romantic Times BOOKreviews*
on *Touching Midnight*

*Available the first week of May 2008
wherever books are sold!*

**MIRA**®

# REQUEST YOUR
# FREE BOOKS!

## 2 FREE NOVELS
## FROM THE ROMANCE/SUSPENSE
## COLLECTION PLUS 2 FREE GIFTS!

**YES!** Please send me 2 FREE novels from the Romance/Suspense Collection and my 2 FREE gifts (gifts are worth about $10). After receiving them, if I don't wish to receive any more books, I can return the shipping statement marked "cancel." If I don't cancel, I will receive 4 brand-new novels every month and be billed just $5.49 per book in the U.S. or $5.99 per book in Canada, plus 25¢ shipping and handling per book plus applicable taxes, if any*. That's a savings of at least 20% off the cover price! I understand that accepting the 2 free books and gifts places me under no obligation to buy anything. I can always return a shipment and cancel at any time. Even if I never buy another book from the Reader Service, the two free books and gifts are mine to keep forever.

185 MDN EF5Y   385 MDN EF6C

| | |
|---|---|
| Name | (PLEASE PRINT) |

| | |
|---|---|
| Address | Apt. # |

| | | |
|---|---|---|
| City | State/Prov. | Zip/Postal Code |

Signature (if under 18, a parent or guardian must sign)

### Mail to **The Reader Service:**
**IN U.S.A.:** P.O. Box 1867, Buffalo, NY 14240-1867
**IN CANADA:** P.O. Box 609, Fort Erie, Ontario L2A 5X3

Not valid to current subscribers to the Romance Collection,
the Suspense Collection or the Romance/Suspense Collection.

**Want to try two free books from another line?**
**Call 1-800-873-8635 or visit www.morefreebooks.com.**

* Terms and prices subject to change without notice. N.Y. residents add applicable sales tax. Canadian residents will be charged applicable provincial taxes and GST. Offer not valid in Quebec. This offer is limited to one order per household. All orders subject to approval. Credit or debit balances in a customer's account(s) may be offset by any other outstanding balance owed by or to the customer. Please allow 4 to 6 weeks for delivery. Offer available while quantities last.

**Your Privacy:** Harlequin is committed to protecting your privacy. Our Privacy Policy is available online at www.eHarlequin.com or upon request from the Reader Service. From time to time we make our lists of customers available to reputable third parties who may have a product or service of interest to you. If you would prefer we not share your name and address, please check here. ☐

BOB08R

# nocturne™

## THE FINAL INSTALLMENT OF
## THE BLOODRUNNERS TRILOGY

## Last Wolf Watching

Runner Brody Carter has found his match in
Michaela Doucet, a human with unusual psychic powers.
When Michaela's brother is threatened, Brody becomes
her protector, and suddenly not only has to protect her
from her enemies but also from himself....

## LOOK FOR
# LAST WOLF WATCHING
## BY
# RHYANNON
# BYRD

*Available May 2008 wherever you buy books.*

**Dramatic and Sensual Tales of Paranormal Romance**

www.eHarlequin.com          SN61786

# TONI ANDREWS

32365 BEG FOR MERCY          ___ $6.99 U.S. ___ $8.50 CAN.

*(limited quantities available)*

| | |
|---|---|
| TOTAL AMOUNT | $ _____ |
| POSTAGE & HANDLING | $ _____ |
| ($1.00 FOR 1 BOOK, 50¢ for each additional) | |
| APPLICABLE TAXES* | $ _____ |
| TOTAL PAYABLE | $ _____ |

*(check or money order—please do not send cash)*

To order, complete this form and send it, along with a check or money order for the total above, payable to MIRA Books, to: **In the U.S.:** 3010 Walden Avenue, P.O. Box 9077, Buffalo, NY 14269-9077; **In Canada:** P.O. Box 636, Fort Erie, Ontario, L2A 5X3.

Name: _____
Address: _____ City: _____
State/Prov.: _____ Zip/Postal Code: _____
Account Number (if applicable): _____

075 CSAS

*New York residents remit applicable sales taxes.
*Canadian residents remit applicable GST and provincial taxes.

**MIRA**®

www.MIRABooks.com          MTA0508BL